Blessings
FROM DA HOOD

Philip Allisson

NEWMAN SPRINGS PUBLISHING
320 Broad Street
Red Bank, NJ 07701

First originally published by Newman Springs Publishing 2022

ISBN 978-1-63881-237-1 (Paperback)
ISBN 978-1-63881-238-8 (Digital)

Printed in the United States of America

To those who live the thug life and to those
who have been redeemed from the life.

Chapter 1

Rubin Jackson has just gotten out of jail. He is a high school dropout and a gang member who just did a two-year stretch for dealing drugs. Rubin is black, five feet ten, and weighs 175 pounds. He is twenty-one years old and back out on the streets again. Born and raised on the streets of South Central, Los Angeles, and unable to stay out of trouble, he goes back to his gang. Rubin knocks on the door of the house where the gang leader lives. Rod opens the door.

"Yo, what's up GI?" Rod says. Rubin's nickname is GI because of his U.S. Marine Corps-style haircut.

Rod gives Rubin a handshake followed by a hug.

"Another nigga in the house! Waz up, GI?" Cruz says. He gives Rubin a hug. "Good to see ya back from your vacation."

"Yo, Snake!" Cruz calls out. "Look who's back!"

Snake stands in the doorway. Snake is six feet two and weighs 225 pounds of solid muscle. He has big arms, chest, and big legs. He is wearing a yellow LA Lakers tank top and is holding a beer in his hand.

"Mother fu…" Snake starts to say.

"It's me, cuz," Rubin says. Snake, whose real name is Jamal Jackson, is Rubin's cousin. They both started the gang together. They now have a name for the gang. They call themselves the Super Destroyers.

Both Jamal and Rubin have been in trouble with the law since the eighth grade. Snake's father died in a car wreck when Snake was in the fourth grade. His mother has not been the same since and never got over his death. She looked for all the things that she could do to make the pain of the loss go away. But she looked in all the wrong places. She had known him since high school and got married

1

just after they graduated. But she still holds the pain inside. She grew up in a Baptist church. But because of what happened, she blamed God for everything and became very bitter towards God. She became an alcoholic and just did not care about life anymore.

"God could call you home anytime," her pastor would tell her. But she could not understand the pain and hurt that she felt when her pastor said that to her.

Rubin's father left after he was born. His father was a crackhead who killed somebody for money to buy crack and died in prison from a shank to his heart. His mother tried to raise Rubin the right way. Rubin was closer to his cousin Snake than his mother and became rebellious to his mother and to society.

The influence that Snake has on Rubin has been a very negative one. Snake got Rubin into drugs and crime in eighth grade, and things have gotten worse since then. They both have been in and out of jail since tenth grade.

"So wat up, GI?" Snake asks. "When did you get out?"

"Today, man. Gimme a blunt," Rubin says.

"Nah, sorry, G. Them niggas smoked it all."

"For real?"

Snake turns to Lizard and Scorpion. Lizard and Scorpion are two other gang members who always has drugs on them that anyone can buy. They are sitting in the corner of the room on the sofa, playing kung fu on each other with their hands.

"You stole my rice. You, you, you," Scorpion says with a deep Chinese voice.

"Oh yeah? You stole my Cho Mein soup!" Lizard says, also with a deep Chinese voice.

"I will kill you with my kung fu lizard style!"

"I'm gonna kill you with my scorpion kung fu!"

"Hey yo!" Snake says. "I'm gonna kung fu both you niggas if my cousin don't get anything to smoke tonight."

"Yo, word up," Lizard says. "Give the homey something." Lizard turns to Scorpion. "Yo man, you a greedy nigga."

"Greedy nothing," Scorpion says. He reaches into his shirt pocket and pulls out a dime bag of marijuana. "I bring the weed. You bring the rest. Welcome back, bro."

Lizard looks up at Rubin. "Welcome back too, GI."

"Thanks, bro," Rubin says.

"You on probation, GI?" Lizard asks.

"Yeah," Rubin says. "For two years."

"Then what you doing smoking weed for?"

"That's my business. If I wanna smoke weed, then I gonna smoke weed."

"Ight. Don't be looking for me when you get busted for it."

"Besides that. They ain't gonna find out."

Scorpion and Lizard go back to what they are doing. Rubin goes into Snake's room with Snake to smoke a joint. He picks up a Wu Tang Clan CD and puts it in the CD player and hits play on the CD player. Then he sits on Snake's bed.

"So what's been going down since I been gone?" Rubin asks.

"Ain't no different than before," Snake says. "Mama still drunk and don't care. She ain't here tonight. She gone out with Betty tonight. You still got 5-0 coming out here busting us for something. Last week, they came by looking for you. I told them you were in jail, and they still want to mess with us just because we black."

"Just give 'em a donut, and they leave," Rubin says.

Snake laughs and then gets serious. "I'm glad you got out today. We in big trouble with the Majestics."

"Why'z dat?"

"They blame us for getting them busted on drugs."

"How?"

"Cruz and I were hanging in the park with them while they were playing basketball. Me and Cruz was just hanging out waiting to get into the next game. After the game, we offered them to buy some weed. The 5-0 pulled up and busted half of 'em, and Cruz and me split. We ran, jumped the fence, and got into his car and split. We didn't know 5-0 was watching us.

"Them Majestics did three drive-bys on us last week. They think that they got Cruz because they shot a nigga who look like 'em.

Now they after the rest of us. They pulled a drive-by on my house last night. Good thing I was in the bathroom, or else I would have been dead. Lizard almost got shot."

"When did all this start?"

"About three weeks ago. Rods our look out tonight."

"Who the dude that look like Cruz dat got shot?"

"I don't know. Some nigga who goes by Applehead. Some crack-head. He's still in the hospital in ICU. He was on crack when he got shot. Cops thought they were after 'em."

"Why waz he at your house? Buying crack?"

"Yeah. He was buying some crack from Lizard. The nigga looked just like Cruz."

Rubin holds the dime bag of weed with his thumb and index finger and starts to think.

"Snake man," Rubin says.

"Yo."

"I been thinking man. Been doing a lot of thinking while I was in jail. I mean jail got me thinking about a lot about my life, man."

"Man, what the hell jail got you thinking about?"

Rubin holds up the dime bag of weed in front of himself with two fingers.

"This," Rubin says.

"What about it? Smoke it, G. You afraid or something? Quitting?"

"Nah man. It's not the weed. It's what we been doing. I mean it's what I been doing for the past ten years. I mean with our lives. One night, when I was laying on my bunk, my whole life flashed in front of my face. Is this what we gonna do for the rest of our lives?"

"Nigga, what's wrong with you? What we doing?"

"Gangbanging."

"Yo. What about it, man? You giving up on me?"

"I mean, I heard some preacher talking about it while I was in jail."

"T. D. Jakes?"

"Nah. Some other nigga. He waz talking about how thug life is Satan's way of niggas killing niggas. With drive-by shootings, crack, and all that thug life. I tried to pay no mind to it. But the nigga made sense."

"Man, don't be listening to it. That nigga just wants you to diss your homeboys. Besides, if he's talking about God, you know that he's getting you to diss your boys for money. Don't listen to his..."

"Yo, the preacher made sense, Snake."

"So what you gonna do? Become born-again and be a preacher? This is your life, nigga. You are born-again into a deadly gangbanger in my image. I created you into what you are. And don't you forget it, GI. We started this thing together, we ain't gonna end it. SUPER DESTROYER FOR LIFE!"

Snake puts up his gang sign on his hands. "We ain't got time to walk out now. We got them Majestics niggas on us now, and you ain't backing out on me! Not today! Not ever!"

"Well..." Rubin tries to speak.

There is a knock on Snake's bedroom door. Cruz is opening the door slowly to come in. As he is pushing slowly, he is also knocking.

"Yo, G," Cruz says. "There's someone here to see ya in the living room."

Rubin stands up. "What, my probation officer? Or some cop?"

"Dude, just chill and come and see," Cruz says.

Rubin walks out of the bedroom and goes into the living room. A girl stands up and gives him a big hug. It's Jackie, Rubin's long-time girlfriend. They both stand in the living room with their arms around each other and kissing.

"Yo, you taking up all the space in the living room," Rod says. "Get a room."

Rubin and Jackie let go of each other.

"Hey man," Rubin says. "I ain't held my baby in two years."

Right after Rubin says that, a Ford Mustang pulls up to the front of Snake's house. Three guys with ski masks lean out the window while one sits on the door of the front passenger door with AK-47s and open fire on the house. Bullets are flying everywhere. Everybody drops to the floor. Rod sticks his hand out the door of Snake's house with a .45 Magnum and begins to open fire at the guys in the car, not seeing if he hit any of the gunmen in the car. After about forty-five seconds of gunfire and cuss words, it's over.

Snake gets to his knees and shouts, "Is everybody okay?"

Everybody gets up. Jackie remains on the floor face down in a pool of blood.

"JACKIE!" Rubin cries out. He runs to her body on the floor and kneels down. "No!" Trying to wake her up, he pushes her body with his hands. He turns her on to her back. Jackie lies there on her back with her blood coming out of her mouth, stomach, and head. Blood is all over the carpet. Then it hits Rubin that the love of his life is dead.

Chapter 2

Sirens are going off. Jackie's body is in a body bag and is lying on a stretcher. The paramedics put her in an ambulance and drive away.

Jackie Sinclair was a longtime girlfriend of Rubin. She is eighteen years old and has just finished high school. While Rubin was in jail, he encouraged her to stay in school. Jackie was an honor student and was getting set to go to Rutgers University for a bachelor's degree in business, a future business woman with potential. Now dead with four bullets in her body. Four powerful slugs killed her instantly.

"Who did this?" Officer Hanson asked. Officer Dereck Hanson is an Irish American cop who has been assigned to the gang unit of LAPD for seven years. He is asking questions about the shooting.

"I don't know," Rubin says.

"Did anyone see anything?" Officer Hanson asks.

Nobody says anything.

"If nobody talks, you're just gonna make it harder on yourselves."

"I saw a blue car, and the niggas in the car had on ski masks," Rod says.

"Did you get a tag number?"

"I said that's all I saw. How you cops expect me to see who it was, you big fat jelly-donut-eating mother..."

"Hey!" Officer Hanson interrupts. "I'm just here to help you guys!"

Snake puts his right arm over Rubin's shoulder and says, "Yo. All I know is that a few stupid niggas drove by, shot up my house, and killed my cousin's girlfriend and got away. And nobody seen nothing."

"Ain't nobody know who they are," Rubin says.

"Hey, look," Officer Hanson says. "You had a drive-by here last night. You had a person who got shot last week. Something is up, and you better tell me what's going on. You better tell me who is after you guys."

"Ain't nobody is after us. Drive-bys happen in the hood every day," Snake says.

"Well, nobody does it unless they have reason to," Officer Hanson says.

"Unit L923," Hanson's CB radio went off. "Please assist a nineteen at Twenty-Fourth Street and Main."

Hanson walks over his car and grabs his CB.

"Ten-four. Unit LA923 now moving in."

Hanson turns to the rest of the gang and says, "Don't try to undo this yourselves, or you'll just get into more trouble with the law. So sit back and let the police handle this." Hanson gets into his car and leaves.

The gang goes back into Snakes house.

"I can't believe that they killed my girl. I can't believe they killed her!" Rubin cries out.

"Yo. We tried to reason with them. Them niggas are gonna pay now," Snake says. "They hurt one of us, they hurt *all* of us!" Snake shouts.

"Yo man, let's go there and destroy 'em all!" Rod says. He takes out his .45 and changes the clip with a full one. "We are gonna live up to our name, Super Destroyers. You with us GI? They just killed your girl."

"Yeah. I'm in," GI says.

"Good. You were about to quit on us. I told you. You in it for life. I'm gonna call Toad and Centipede and have 'em hook up with us later."

Rubin wakes up the next morning in his own bed. Waking up in his own bed is a great feeling and a sign of relief. It is better than sleeping on a hard jail cell mattress and a hard metal bottom just four inches under him with a little flat pillow. He lies there face up, looking at the ceiling. It's eleven in the morning. He just lies there, thinking about the night before. He keeps seeing Jackie getting shot and killed right in front of him and her body lying there dead. He was so much in love with her. He had planned to buy her an engagement ring and proposing to her when he got out of jail. Now, dead in his arms, the night he got out of jail. A beautiful life that only God can give now taken away because of a drive-by. Tears begin to roll down Rubin's face.

"Why?" Rubin asks himself. "Why her and not me? That bullet was meant for me. I should be dead instead."

This is the first time that someone close to him has died in his arms.

"Oh Lord," he says. The Lord is the last person that he wants to talk to. Rubin never goes to church. He was baptized when he was a baby, but he never received Jesus Christ as his Savior.

"Lord, why did she have to die? It should have been me. Why wasn't it me?"

The tears just keeps rolling down his face. Then the landline phone rings. But he lets it ring until the answering machine picked up. He hears his mother's voice come on and say, "Hello. You have reached the Jacksons. Please leave a message after the tone and I will get back to you." After the machine made the beep, he hears someone's voice leaving a message.

"Hey yo, GI. This is Cruz. Just calling ya ta see if you ight. Call me later." Then Cruz hangs up.

He gets out of bed, wipes his tears off his face, and gets ready to take a shower. After he showers, he gets dressed. He checks his answering machine for another message. It shows that it has another message. He hits play. The message says, "Hey, Rubin. This is Kristal. I heard that you just got out last night. Cruz told me, and I can't believe what happened to Jackie. Call me if you want to talk. My phone number is 552-2936. Bye."

Rubin picks up the phone and calls Kristal. Kristal is Jackie's best friend. She is one friend whom you can count on to be there for you. Anybody could talk to her, and she would not gossip your business to anyone. She is also close friends with Rubin since high school.

After a few rings, a girl's voice answers the phone.

"Hello?" says the voice.

"Yo, what's up Krystal? This is GI," Rubin says.

"Rubin!" says Kristal. "How's it going? Are you okay?"

"No," Rubin answers. "Not doing too good. Can't get it out of my head. I keep seeing Jackie on the floor. I even had a dream about it last night."

"I was in tears when I got the news from Cruz this morning. When I stopped crying, I called you."

"She died in my arms last night."

"Do you know who did this?"

"Rod put his hand out the door to shoot. But all he saw were some niggas with some ski masks."

"Do you know what gang did this? Who is responsible for this?"

"It could be any gang."

"Are you in trouble with any other gangs?"

"Do we have to talk about this right now? Let's meet up somewhere."

"Yeah. Why don't we do that? Can you meet me over at my church say around three thirty? I have to do something for my pastor today."

"Yeah. Let's meet at your church. Not that I don't want to go to church. But I'll do it to talk to you. What church is it?"

"It's called Holy Revival over on Second Avenue right up the street from the 7-Eleven. You will see a big sign that says Holy Revival Ministries. You can't miss it. Meet me there at three thirty?"

"Yeah. I'll see you at three thirty. I'll see you then and we can talk."

They both hang up.

Rubin arrives at the church at three thirty by walking. He walks up the church stairs to the doors. The church is a big red brick building that has a traditional stained glass windows and a church bell on top. Rubin opens the door of the church and walks in.

A creepy feeling comes over him, a feeling that he doesn't want to be there. He suddenly feels like someone is watching him. He walks down the center isle between the wooden pews. He still has the same sick feeling that whoever is watching him is right behind him.

"Hi, Rubin," Kristal says as she got up from her knees, praying at the altar.

Rubin gets so scared that he takes out his .45 Magnum and points it at her.

"Rubin! It's me, Kristal!" she exclaims with fear.

Kristal is black with shoulder-length hair. She was a track star in high school, now twenty years old and serving in the church full-time. She is five feet three inches tall with a skinny body, and can sing with a beautiful voice.

Rubin puts the gun down and lets out a sigh of relief. Then he puts the gun back in his pants. They walk up to each other and embrace with a hug for a minute.

"Are you okay?" Kristal asks. "You don't need a gun in here. There ain't anyone in here who will kill you."

They let go of each other.

"I'm ight. I got this gun from Scorpion today, little welcome home gift. He knew that I had to walk here and didn't want me to walk unarmed."

"You should have told me that you had to walk. I would have picked you up. I got my mom's car with me."

"Oh. I hope I didn't scare you."

"It's okay. Just keep that thing out of sight. If Pastor David walks in here and sees that thing, you could get into some serious trouble. He has connections with the LAPD."

"Ight. I'll keep it in my pants."

They both sit down on the wooden pew of the front row of the sanctuary.

"How do you feel, Rubin?" she asks.

"I don't know. I feel hurt, angry. I feel like part of me died last night."

"I know. I feel the same way. Do you think the police will ever catch the ones who did this?"

"No. But I will."

"What do you mean *you* will? Don't you know that the Bible says, '"Vengeance is Mine," says the Lord?' And that the Bible also says, 'Touch not My anointed ones?' Rubin, God cares about what happens to his anointed ones."

"What do you mean 'anointed' ones?" Rubin asks.

"She was anointed to sing. She sang in here almost every Sunday. Jackie was a soloist in our church."

Rubin being totally caught off guard asks, "She sang in here?"

"Yes!" she says with a smile. "She and I sang together sometimes also. I taught her how to sing. She didn't tell you?"

"No. I never knew that she went to church. She came to see me while I was in jail even on Sundays."

"I know she did. She always came after service. But now I know that she is going to be with Jesus forever. She fell in love with Jesus so much when she got saved."

"She got 'saved'? What that mean?"

"Saved, meaning that she accepted Jesus Christ into her heart and became born-again. I am telling you, she is dancing around the throne room and singing for God right now."

"Well then, if she is, heaven is a better place to be than here. I am glad at least she got out of the thug life. I didn't want her in it any more while I was in jail."

"Yeah. Both my parents warned me about the gang life. My dad, even though he's not saved, told me that it is not good to get involved in gangs. You know that you can still get out of it."

"I don't know about me. I want to get them niggas who shot Jackie first. Then maybe get out."

"Rubin. Why do you have that kind of attitude? Let God deal with these people who killed Jackie."

"Yo! God ain't gonna do nothing! Since when did God ever do anything for me?"

"God saved Jackie and got her out of the gang life."

"Well, he did that for her. What about me?" Rubin stands up and points his thumb at his chest.

"God ain't done nothing good for me. My dad left me when I was born. I would always hope and pray that he would come home. I also prayed that my mom would find a man who would take care of us and be my dad. My mom would find a man who would drink and beat her. I prayed that he would go to church, but he would drink instead and died in a car crash. I prayed that I would never go to jail, and I been there so many times. I prayed that I never would join a gang, and I did. I helped found the Super Destroyers with Snake. I prayed that Jackie would never die, and look what happened to her.

"God hates me! That's what I think. God hates me! He's just waiting to throw me into hell!"

"But Rubin, you never got to know His son Jesus. When was the last time you sent to church?"

"Church never did me any good to go. So why bother with it?"

"Hey! What's all this shouting going on in here? I thought I was preaching tonight," Pastor David Blanchard says as he walked into the sanctuary from behind the church.

Pastor David Blanchard is a tall black man and in his early fifties. He has been the pastor of Holy Revival for nineteen years. He is well respected by his members. He has ten other pastors under his leadership. He and his wife started the church in his living room of his home in LA.

He has a large gang outreach with a former gang members running the ministry. Pastor Blanchard has been like a bright light for all gangs in the area to see, and many have been drawn to the light that he shines. Pastor Blanchard was also a former gang leader who did time in prison for murder and other gang-related crimes. He accepted Jesus Christ in his heart while in prison at San Quinton.

After he served twenty years, he was paroled for good conduct and also preached in prison, leading many other inmates to Christ. When he got out, he met his wife and started a Bible study together in their living room, and after about a year, it became a church. It has expanded over the years and has become what it is today. The biggest problem that he has always had was parking. His church grew so much that there were no more parking anymore. In order to get a good seat, people had to get to church early.

Pastor Blanchard walks up to Rubin and extends his hand out to greet Rubin.

"Hello, young man," Pastor Blanchard says to Rubin. "Is that you who was preaching just now?"

"Hey yo. What's up old man?" Rubin says as he puts his fist into Pastor Blanchard's hand, expecting a fist bump.

"Hi, pastor," Kristal says. "This is Rubin Jackson. He was a friend of Jackie."

"Well, hello Rubin," pastor says. "What can we do for you?"

"I'm straight. You can call me GI like everyone else."

"Very well. You can call me Pastor David like everybody else. So you're GI. I've heard about you."

"Yeah? Well, I was just leaving. Later, Kris," Rubin says then gave her a hug.

Rubin walks up the isle and out the door of the church.

"That was Jackie's boyfriend," Kristal says to Pastor David. "He's not saved and just got out of jail last night. Jackie was with him when she was shot."

"Oh that's right," Pastor David says. "Jackie and you told me that he was in jail. I didn't know that his two years was up. Now that Jackie is with the Lord, how is he taking it?"

"Not good at all. He has a lot of anger and hatred in himself."

"Well, I will be praying for him. How are you taking it?"

"Not so good, I guess. I know that she is with Jesus, but I know that I'm gonna miss her so much. She was my best friend."

"Death does pay a toll on everybody. I've seen too much of it when I was in the gang. But now we have to understand that those who die in Christ will live forever in the kingdom of God. I sure wish that I could go back and bring those who I have killed while I was in the gang and bring them out of where they are right now."

"I know."

Chapter 3

Two houses down from where Rubin lives is where his best friend T-Pot lives. T-Pot got his nickname by smoking crack through a tea kettle. His real name is Sam Stewart. He had to commit a crime to become a member of the gang while some other gang members had to take beatings from five other guys in the gang. Some other members had to commit some serious crimes to get in, in order to show their worthiness to be called a Super Destroyer.

The colors of the Super Destroyers are red and black. The red stands for the blood that they shed of the people that they killed. The black stands for the evil in themselves.

Over at T-Pot's house, Rubin is in T-Pot's room listening to some rap music.

"Yo, G, you were where?" T-Pot asks.

"I was in church," Rubin answers.

"Church? Man, don't be getting religious on me now, nigga. What's wrong wit' you?"

"Chill, man. I was just talking with Kristal Jenkins. You know, Jackie's best friend. She was trying to preach Jesus to me."

"Nah, man. Don't be believing none of her jazz."

"I heard a lot about Jesus while I was in jail. It didn't hurt me to hear some. The preacher man was saying dat some seeds were planted. But what does dat mean?"

"Hey, nigga, speaking of seeds, I got some weed seed right here, G. Welcome to Jamaica."

T-Pot holds up a small Ziploc bag of seeds to grow some marijuana.

"My boy over on Main Street just got back from Jamaica. He hooked me up good. I do favor for him, and he shook me up free. We can plant these and make some of our own money. I also got some real weed in my pocket. Want some? On me."

"Nah, man. I shouldn't be smoking it. I'm on probation. Gotta take a piss test every week."

"Ight. More for me. What you wanna do now, G?"

"I'm headed up to Jackie's folk's home and see waz up."

"Hey, I go wit' you."

"Yeah, come on, man. Don't be smoking not'ing over there. Them people religious and don't like us."

"Cause we gangsta?"

"Yeah."

"Oh man. Discrimination."

"Yeah. A real blessing from the hood."

Rubin and T-Pot walk out the door and up the street for a few blocks and turn right. They walk to the second house and up the steps. Rubin knocks on the window of the front door. Jackie's father opens the door. He stands inside the house holding the door as it opens from the inside.

"Oh. It's you," Mr. Sinclair says. "You come here to cause more trouble?"

"No, sir," Rubin says. "Just coming to pay my respects to ya."

"Well, I don't need 'em! Now get the hell off my property before I call the police."

"Hey, man," Rubin says. "I just got out of jail last night. I didn't know that this was gonna happen. I quit smoking weed, and I am on probation."

"Yeah?" Mr. Sinclair asks. "But you got that gang to make you feel important. Now, I thought I said to get off my property!" Mr. Sinclair orders and slams the door on Rubin and T-Pot.

"Man," T-Pot said. "Dat nigga rude."

"Let's chill over at my crib," Rubin said.

"Ight. We call him later."

Jackie's father is a tall black man with a bald head. He is in his late fifties. He and Jackie's mother are both born-again Christians and members of Holy Revival. He is known as Big A. His real name is Alex Sinclair. Some people call him Big A or BA because of his six-foot-five and 270-pound body. He was a former defensive end at USC and about to become a top draft pick for the NFL until a car accident ruined his knees for the rest of his life.

"Who was at the door, Alex?" Mrs. Sinclair asked.

"That was that punk GI and one of his homeboys."

"I don't want any of them at Jackie's funeral. If it was not for them, Jackie would still be alive today to continue the Lord's work."

"Well, that's fine with me, baby. I hate them all. May they all burn in hell!"

Back at Rubin's house, Rubin and T-Pot are watching the news on TV. While they are watching the news, they see the story of Jackie's death. Rubin's mother comes home from work and walks into the living room where Rubin and T-Pot are watching TV.

"Now there you go again," Rubin's mother says. "You went and got your own girlfriend shot up and killed."

"But, Ma, I…" Rubin tries to speak.

"No buts, Rubin. Or should I call you by your punk name, GI? You ain't never gonna change."

Ginalee Jackson, Rubin's mother, is a short woman in her early fifties. She is not a born-again Christian, but she does attend a Baptist church every Christmas and Easter.

"So?" Ginalee asks. "Why did they let you out this time for?"

"Ma," Rubin says. "I'm on probation for two years. I'm straight, ma. Haven't smoked weed since I got locked up. I have to take a drug test every week."

"Okay then," Ginalee says. She begins to lay down the rules. "I want you home before midnight every night even on weekends."

"What?" Rubin asks in disbelief.

"You heard what I said, boy. Don't give me no what. I'm the head nigga in charge now! This is my house. You abide by my rules. If you don't like it, you can move in with one of your punk gangsta homeboys.

"I want you in before midnight every night. You are to clean this house and keep it clean. And I don't want no parties. And keep your ugly, no-good, punk, crackhead, gangsta, homeboys out of my

17

house when I'm not home! Sam, get your shoes off my coffee table. This ain't your living room."

Sam Stewart is T-Pot's real name. He has no manners. He would always come into someone's house and act like he is the owner. He would open the door without knocking and come right in. He would open your refrigerator without asking and take whatever he wanted. He would open the kitchen cupboards looking for food. He would turn on the TV without asking. He would change the channel when someone is watching TV and put it on the BET or porno channel if available. He would also blast someone's stereo with rap music. He would come over and do anything to annoy anyone he can.

If you were sitting down and having a meal, he would put his hands in your plate and steal something to eat. He would also do that in restaurants. He would walk by someone eating, snatch something out of somebody's plate, and shove it in his mouth in less than three seconds and keep walking. He is also an expert at snatching your fork that you are about to put into your mouth and eating what's on the fork.

With other people's drinks, he would walk right up to a table where someone is sitting, grab their glass, and guzzle it down as fast as he can and not care if he was spilling anything. If anyone ever stood up to him, T-Pot would pull out his .45 Magnum to their faces.

T-Pot got into the gang by committing armed robbery. He was ordered by Snake to rob a 7-Eleven. He went to a 7-Eleven wearing a ski mask with his .45 Magnum in hand. He went in after midnight. He put the gun to the cashier's head and demanded the money from the register. He had staked out the place for a week, getting to know the layout of the 7-Eleven, and found out when the best time to go in to rob the store. When he went in, he was the only person in the store other than the cashier. It took T-Pot one minute to rob the store and ran out with five hundred dollars before shooting the cashier. The cashier survived the gunshot, and the Super Destroyers had a new member.

"Hey yo," Rubin says. "I've seen enough of this. I'm in the mood for a game."

"Ight. What you wanna play?"

Rubin gets up and puts in a Mortal Kombat game into his Play Station and turns on the game system. He gives T-Pot a game controller and grabs the other. They watch the story of the game. Rubin hits the start button on the game controller. They both choose their characters that they want to be.

"Man, I been in jail fo long, I don't know if I can still drop your punk nappy head," Rubin says.

"Shut up, nigga. You never dropped me once. I can still drop you. I beat the game."

"Man, I used to beat you all the time. You ain't nothin', nigga."

They start to play the game.

Rubin and T-Pot go at it. They both go back and forth on the TV screen fighting each other. Rubin gives T-Pot and uppercut and wins the match.

"Yeah! That's it. I dropped you punk nappy nigga."

"Nah, nah, nah, nigga. The game ain't over yet. Still got another fight."

The phone rings and Ginalee answers it.

"Hello? Yeah. Hold on."

"Rubin, it's for you."

She gives Rubin the cordless phone.

"Yeah, what's up? Who dis?" He presses the Start button on the game controller to pause the game.

"Hey, GI, what's up? This is Kristal."

"Yo, what's up Kristal?"

"I'm calling you from church."

"Church? What? You trying to convert me now?"

"No, GI. I'm calling you because my church is having a picnic next Saturday at the park on Fifth Avenue, and I am inviting you to it. It's the park over on Fifth Avenue right up the street from the church. Would you like to go? Can you make it on Saturday around eleven in the morning?"

"Yeah. I can go. I'll be there on Saturday. Right now, I am playing a game. Call you later."

Back at the church, Kristal hangs up the phone.

"What did he say?" Pastor David asks.

"He said that he's coming. What if he brings his gang?"

"That is what we are about. We have a gang outreach. Let the Lord do His work. 'Trust in the Lord, and lean not on your own understanding. In all your ways, acknowledge Him, and He will direct your path,' says Proverbs 3:5–6."

*****

After they played a few rounds of Mortal Kombat, they go to Snake's house. Snake is shocked at what Rubin and T-Pot are saying about going to the church picnic.

"Nigga, are you stupid?" Snake asks Rubin.

"Man, waz up with you?" Rubin asks.

"That's the park where it got started with the Majesties," Snake answers. "That's where they hang out. They be always playing ball there. Ah man, why you do that fo?"

"Yo Snake," T-Pot interrupts. "How bout we all go wit' him? I don't want my nigga to go down without us. He already gave his word that he was going. You made da rule dat if one nigga go down, we all go down together. You were the one who made dat rule."

"Ight then," Snake says. "We all meet at my house, and we all be strapped! Then we go together."

Chapter 4

It is Saturday morning. All members of the Super Destroyers are at Snake's house. Five members get into Toad's car.

Toad has been with the gang since high school. He is twenty years old. He stands at six feet four and weighs 250 pounds of solid muscle. He has played linebacker in high school, but he was influenced by Snake to join the Super Destroyers after he saw his girlfriend get killed in a drive-by shooting at her cousin's house.

Toad got into the Super Destroyers by purposely getting pulled over by an LAPD rookie police officer for speeding in a dark alleyway road in a stolen car. When the police officer came up to Toad's window, Toad pulled out his .44 Magnum and fired the gun at point-blank range at the officer's head and killed him instantly. Toad got out of his car. He then picked up the dead police officer, put the officer back in his patrol car, and set it on fire. When backup had arrived, Toad was gone. The next night, Snake had given Toad a welcoming party. Toad never got caught and there was no evidence to link Toad to the crime.

The gang always gave Toad a feeling of security and acceptance. His parents abandoned him when he was nine years old. He was raised by his uncle who later died of a heroin overdose when he was in high school. Having no positive role model, he became good friends with Snake.

Centipede, Chris Barley, is Toad's best friend. He is sitting in the front seat of Toad's Lincoln. Toad and Centipede live in the same house. Centipede was born in Haiti. He has dreads and speaks with a Haitian accent. He is six feet one and weighs about two hundred pounds. Centipede was also on the same high school football team with Toad. He played strong safety.

Toad was the one who influenced him to get into the gang. When Centipede met Snake, Snake had made him burn a chain of townhouses. The fire and destruction damage was about millions of dollars. Twelve people were killed, and thirty people were seriously burned. The next night, a party was given to Centipede to welcome him into the Super Destroyers. Both Toad and Centipede moved up in rank in the gang because of their acts and willingness to commit crimes. They were both second-in-command next to Snake and GI.

Other members of the Super Destroyers who are in Toad's car are Sticker, Flicker, and Dragon. Toad's younger brother Sticker was blessed into the gang by Snake and GI. Sticker had a reputation of pulling out his knives and sticking them into other gangbangers of other gangs when Snake needed someone to shed blood for an act of revenge. Sticker had only been living in South Central LA for a few years after moving from Haiti. He had stabbed a few people in Haiti and came to the U.S. to get away with it.

Flicker, Joseph Emanuel, is another Haitian. He is a cousin of Toad. He was also blessed into the gang just for being a family member of Toad and Sticker. Nobody is sure how he got the name Flicker.

Dragon, David Brown, is one of the newest members of the Super Destroyers. He got his reputation by being an arsonist of cars, houses, and apartment buildings. He calls himself Dragon because he feels that all he has to do is just breathe, and something will catch on fire. Dragon is twenty years old, black, and has a bald head. He is five feet eleven and weighs 180 pounds. After Snake found out about Dragon being an arsonist, he blessed him into the Super Destroyers right away.

The rest of the Super Destroyers are in Snake's Dodge van. All members of the Super Destroyers are armed and ready.

The park is about the size of three football fields wide. Holy Revival Ministries set up a stage right in the middle of the park. The weather is great, eighty-five degrees and sunny skies with no clouds, just perfect for a church picnic revival. The park has tennis courts, swimming pools, swings, and a jungle gym for children. The park has a few basketball courts that are about fifty yards from the stage that Holy Revival set up. Picnic tables are set up in the shade just ten yards in front of the stage.

It is ten in the morning, and Holy Revival's choir is on stage opening up the picnic with the song "Stomp." The worship leader, Anthony Johnson, is singing the lead.

Anthony Johnson is a former gang leader. He started his own gang called Northside Central Bullies. He accepted Christ through Pastor David Blanchard.

Everybody is having a great time dancing and worshiping the Lord. After a few minutes, the song is over. Anthony starts preaching.

"I used to be a gang leader. But praise the Lord, I'm saved! When I think of the goodness of Jesus and all that he has done for me, my soul! Hallelujah! My soul! Look at somebody next to you and say, 'My soul.' My soul cries hallelujah! Jesus! Thank you for saving me!"

The church band goes wild with a fast praise and worship interlude music for a minute. It sends the congregation dancing and worshiping. Anthony has a reason to give God glory. He was in and out of prison. He was involved with drive-by shootings and many other gang-related crimes. Anthony is now a born-again spirit-filled Christian. He now runs the gang outreach ministry in Holy Revival.

When the music stops, Anthony grabs the microphone and says, "I was looking for acceptance. I was looking for love. I was looking for a fix to all my problems. I thought the gang would be it. I wanted to be the life of the party. I loved all the attention and power that it gave me. I thought that drive-by shootings was the only way to get even with someone. But all that anger, bitterness, and hatred sent me to ten years in prison!"

By this time, GI is already at the park. Kristal has told him where to go the night before. GI, Snake, Rod, Lizard, Scorpion, T-Pot, and Cruz meet up with Kristal. They are all listening to what Anthony is saying. They do not care anymore. Toad is driving around the outer perimeter of the park, looking to see if anyone from the Majestics are around.

Anthony continues to speak.

"For the ten years that I did in prison, not one. Not *one* of my homies ever came to visit me. My homies were phonies. I came out after the ten years that I did to look for them and they were gone. Some were shot and killed, and the rest were also in prison. I came to Holy Revival and met Pastor David Blanchard, and now I'm saved! I realized that having a new life in Jesus Christ is what real life and love is about. So because of Jesus, we're blessed!"

From there, Anthony leads the choir and band into the song, "We're Blessed" by Fred Hammond. After the song is over, Anthony leads the choir into the song "Ancient of Days" and "Jesus Is Alive." After the choir and band stopped singing and playing, he started to speak again.

"Well, go ahead and praise him. Praise him all day and praise him all night. There is much more beauty in Jesus Christ than in any other gang that I have ever seen. Now I would like to introduce the man who made me a disciple, who mentored me. And the one who also took part in changing my whole life around. Put your hands together and please help me welcome Pastor David Joel Blanchard!"

Pastor David comes up to the stage. He grabs the microphone and gives Anthony a big hug. Pastor David turns to the crowd and says, "Thank you, Brother Anthony. Well, go ahead and praise the Lord, all ye saints. Let everything that has breath praise the Lord."

"Man," GI says to Kristal. "Is that what church is all about? 'Praise the Lord' and all that bullsh—"

"Rubin!" Kristal interrupts. "What do you have against that? What, you rather go to them old boring religious churches where you fall asleep and get nothing out of it? This is a real church where Jesus is Lord! That other man who you saw singing and giving his testimony was in a gang just like you."

"That nigga is a sellout," T-Pot says.

"What do you mean a sellout? Nobody was there for him while he was in prison and gone when he got out," Kristal says.

Pastor David continues speaking.

"God is an awesome God, and his love endures forever. I am Pastor David Blanchard, and I welcome all you new visitors to our annual picnic. Turn around and hug about three or four people and tell them that Jesus is here today. Jesus is always with us."

Everybody gives each other a hug. They turn around and face Pastor David. Pastor David continues speaking.

"We had a busy week here at Holy Revival. One of our members was shot and killed this week in a drive-by. So today, I would like to honor her memory. So open up your Bibles to 1 Corinthians. Chapter 15 and from verse 51, we read, 'Behold I shew you a mystery, we shall not all sleep, but we shall all be changed! In a moment, in the twinkling of an eye, at the last trump: for the trumpet shall sound, and the dead shall be raised incorruptible, and we shall be changed! For this corruptible must put on incorruption, and this mortal must put on immorality. So when this corruptible shall have an incorruption, and this mortal shall put on immortality, than shall be brought to pass the saying that is written, "Death is swallowed up in victory."'"

"Oh praise the Lord. Glory to God! O death, where is thy sting?! O grave, where is thy victory?! Jesus has victory over death, hell, and the grave! Jesus wants to give us the victory. That is the verse for today."

Pastor David turns to Anthony, "Brother Anthony, can you please lead us into another song?"

Anthony grabs the microphone from Pastor David. Anthony starts singing.

Meanwhile, Toad is driving around the park. He drives slowly to the basketball courts. He takes the scope off his rifle and looks through it. He pulls the car up to the side of the road and onto the grass and turns down the volume of the music that he is playing in his car stereo. He gets a closer look at the basketball courts. The rest of the passengers remain silent. Toad looks through the scope again. He sees a young black teenager crouching down, holding a basketball in his hands. Two other young black guys are standing over him with their arms in the air as if they are covering him.

The guy with the ball is Buff. He is a member of the Majestics. Buff passes the ball to Hit Man, who is another member of the Majestics. Hit Man dribbles the ball down the court and does a layup to score in the basket.

While Toad is looking through the scope, he sees a few other members of the Majestics on the court. He sees two more Majestics sitting on the grass next to the court, smoking weed. Toad starts up the car and does a U-turn to meet up with Snake.

T-Pot starts to get sick and tired of the church choir singing. He gets up from his seat. He walks to the front of the stage. He raises his arms in the air and opens his hands. The rest of the gang watch.

T-Pot starts waving his arms around.

"Wave your hands in the air," T-Pot says. "Wave them like you just don't care. Sing like a bunch of suckers! All you mother fu…"

Kristal looks in disbelief as T-Pot puts his right hand on his groin, and with the left hand, he holds up his middle finger.

Brother Peter, the head usher, sees this. He walks over to T-Pot and taps him on the shoulder. T-Pot turns around. Peter makes a hand gesture to tell him to leave. T-Pot shoves Peter. Two more ushers come to T-Pot. One of them tells T-Pot that he cannot stay in front of the stage doing obscene gestures like this. The other usher tells him to sit down before he calls the police. Finally, T-Pot goes back to the rest of the gang.

Toad meets up with Snake.

"Yo Snake," Toad says. "Some Majestics are over on the basketball court playing ball."

"Ight then," Snake says. "Just chill out and grab a burger for now."

"Ight cool."

T-Pot walks from table to table. He sees a girl about to put a hotdog in her mouth. T-Pot moves in for the kill. He runs and snatches the hotdog just before she puts it in her mouth. He walks away eating the hotdog. When he finishes eating the hotdog, he snatches a burger from someone else. The choir then starts walking off the stage. T-Pot throws the hamburger at one of the ladies in the choir in the head. Nobody sees the burger coming. She gets startled and slips on her robe and lands on her arm. The lady behind her trips over and falls on her face. T-Pot stands there, laughing at the ladies who fall down. He hates church people and hates Jesus Christ.

Both ladies got up slowly with some help from some of the other ladies in the choir. The one who fell on her face got up with blood coming out of her nose. The other lady got up, holding her forearm. She then saw part of her bone sticking out of her arm through the skin. Her husband rushed her to the hospital.

"T-Pot!" Kristal shouts at him. "What in the world is wrong with you? I swear, if I were a gangsta I would blow you away with a shotgun right now!"

"Shut up, hoe!" Snake yells at her. "I want all my niggas over here right now."

The gang regrouped. Snake gives his plan.

"Yo, GI, you just got out," Snake says. "You stay here and we go. Ight? I ain't gonna see you go back to jail."

"Ight," Rubin said. "But you stay too. I don't want to see you go to jail either."

"You right. You stay, I stay. Toad, Centipede, Lizard, and Dragon go. T-Pot, you back them up on foot. Run up from behind. I back you up from here. Don't get careless. You dig?"

"Yeah. I dig," says T-Pot.

Toad, Centipede, Lizard, and Dragon get into Toad's car. Toad drives towards the basketball court. He parks the car on the shoulder of the road about fifty feet from the basketball court.

They all get out. Everyone hides behind a tree. They all take out their weapons. Nobody sees them coming. Toad shouts out, "THE SUN ROTATES!" Then he blows his horn. They all open fire at the Majestics.

The Majestics fall to the ground. Buff gets shot in the head and falls to the ground. T-Pot comes running to the scene. He gets within twenty feet. He takes out his .45 Magnum and starts shooting.

Ice, a member of the Majestics, is laying by a basketball pole and sees T-Pot. He grabs his .45 and fires at T-Pot, hitting him in his chest and head. T-Pot falls into a hole in the ground, gets covered with leaves, and dies.

"Nooo!" GI cries out as he sees the bullet go right through his best friend's body. He tries to run; but Snake, Rod, and Sticker grab him and hold him back.

Chapter 5

Ten police cars from the LAPD and five ambulances arrive at the scene. Toad, Centipede, Dragon, Lizard, and Scorpion are long gone. Seven guys from the Majestics are shot. Three are dead; the others are seriously wounded. There is blood all over the basketball court. Ice is still alive and untouched. He drops to the ground just in time to avoid a bullet that is intended for him. The remainder of the Super Destroyers stay at the picnic. They all watch from a distance.

The police start to question Ice. Sergeant Richard Holmes starts to ask Ice a few questions.

"Who did this?" The sergeant asks.

"I don't know. It all happened so fast," Ice says.

"What did you see?"

"I saw a bunch of niggas get out of a Lincoln, and they shot up all my homies."

"What color was the Lincoln?"

"It was a dark color."

"What else can you tell me about the car?"

Ice thinks about it for a minute. "The car had blue tires."

"Did you see the driver? Can you give me a description of anyone?"

"No. I didn't see anyone. They were all hiding behind those trees."

"Do you know of anybody who would do this?"

Ice looked at the ground to think of what to say. Then he says, "No.

Ice knows that it was the Super Destroyers. But he does not say anything because he wanted to get the revenge, not the LAPD. It is always the same way with the Super Destroyers.

"I can't think of anyone who would do this. The car was too far away and I didn't see who shot at us."

Sergeant Holmes gives Ice his business card. "This is my business card. Call me if you have any information about who shot up your boys. This is my direct line."

After about two hours, the police and ambulance clear the area. They never find the body of T-Pot. Ice walks away. He is able to get rid of his gun before the police gets there.

"What?" GI says. "LAPD left T-Pot's body there!"

The rest of the gang at the picnic runs over to where T-Pot's body is.

"Man!" Snake says. "I hate 5-0! Look what they did. Take his body out of there."

*****

Toad parks the car over at Snake's house. Everybody gets out and sits in front of Snake's house on the porch.

"Is anyone hit?" Toad asks. "Everyone ight?"

"Yeah, cool." Dragon says. "I think we got 'em niggas."

"Yeah. I think we did."

GI wakes up with a headache two weeks later. He keeps seeing T-Pot falling to the ground. It starts to hit seeing that his best friend got shot, killed, and forgotten by the LAPD. He starts to have a flashback of when he was in jail.

He sat way in the back of a large room filled with other inmates. In front of the room was a stage where a guest speaker was. The guest speaker was a tall black man with a bald head. He appeared to be the age of thirty-five years old. The guest speaker was telling the inmates about Jesus and gave his testimony of how God delivered him out of the gang lifestyle. GI started to remember something that the guest speaker said.

"The gang life is Satan's way for a black to kill another black. This is going on in America today. It's going on right here in your own backyard. This is what is going on in some of your lives today. Is this what you really want? Is this what you *really* want? Do you want to be dead before you are twenty-five years old? Do you *really* want to see any more of your homeboys dead? Another thing that will also happen to you is a life sentence or end up on death row in San Quinton. Do you *really* want this for your life? Do you want your children to get killed? Or how about your wife or girlfriends getting killed? Is this what you want? I have seen enough. Not just violence. I have seen enough death! Is this what you *really* want?"

The voice became louder in his head as he lay there. GI started to ask himself, *Is this what I really want?*

He just lies there, looking up at the fan that is above his head. He starts to remember how Jackie was shot and killed. Then he remembers how T-Pot got shot and killed. Rubin asks himself again, *Is this what I really want? Do I really want to stay in this lifestyle anymore? Can God really help me? I will never get to go to Jackie's funeral. I saw my best friend get killed. Who's next?*

Suddenly, the phone rings. He has the portable in his room. The phone rings again.

"Yo, what's up?" Rubin answers.

"Yo. What's up, GI? This is Thomas," the voice on the other end says.

"Who dis?" Rubin asks.

"Thomas. You know, 'Beast.' We met the other night at the club."

"Yo, wat up?"

"Just chilling man. What you doing today?"

"Chilling out with my homies. What you doing?"

"Can I chill with you and your cousin later?"

"Yeah, I guess so," GI looks at his clock on the dresser. "What time?"

"In about an hour?"

"Ight."

GI gives him his address and gets out of bed. He showers and makes breakfast. Just as he finishes breakfast, Cruz comes over. They both sit on the front step of the house.

"How you feeling G?" Cruz asks.

"I feel empty inside. I lost my girlfriend and my best friend. I wonder whose next."

"Look, bro," Cruz says. "Them niggas started this war. So quit worrying. Don't blame yourself. We shot the nigga who killed T-Pot. So what you worried about 'who's next'? Are you worried that you will get shot next? I got your back, G," Cruz pulls up his shirt and shows two of his .45 Magnums.

"I got two .45s. Who say that nothing will happen to you?" Cruz says.

"No. I'm worried one of us will get killed."

"Hey, man. Ain't nobody gonna get killed!"

Just after Cruz said that, a brand-new Mustang GT pulls up in front of the house. Beast gets out of the car and walks to GI and Cruz.

Thomas Pradore is a tall black twenty-one-year-old with a bald head. He is six feet four and weighs 250 pounds. His name fits his character, *Beast*. He is evil to the core. He will kill anyone just for their food.

"Hey yo, G. What's up?" Beast asks. "I got the guns if you got the funds. Where's Snake at? He slither back into his crib?"

"Yo, who's dis nigga?" Cruz asks.

"This is my nigga Beast. He's gonna hook us up," Rubin says.

"Wit' wat?" Cruz asks.

"You'll see," Rubin says.

GI picks up a small rock and throws it across the street, and the rock hits Snake's front door. Snake comes out of his house. He sees Beast. He walks over to Beast.

"Yo, what's up, bro? Snake asks as he gives Beast a fist bump. "Guns and ammo?"

"All here" Beast says. "I just need the dough."

"You live in that house, Snake?" Beast asks, pointing at Snake's house.

"Yeah. That's my house."

"Rumor has it that some nigga got shot in front of your house last month," Beast says.

"Yeah man," Cruz says. "Some nigga named Applehead. He bought some crack from me dat night. Got shot right after he started to leave."

"Rumor also has it that y'all brung T-Pot's dead body to the hospital."

"Yo man," GI says, "where you hear dat from?"

"It don't matter," Beast answers. "Them niggas were my homies. We hung out before. Who shot him?"

"Some gang who calls themselves the Majestics," Snake answers.

"I heard of them. They got some real crooked niggas in that gang," Beast says. "I used to be one of them."

"WHAT?" Snake shouts. Snake pulls out his .9mm and points it at Beast's head.

"You wanna tell me who you are, mother fu…"

GI takes out his .45 Magnum and aims it at Beast's head.

Cruz takes out his .45 Magnum and points it at Beast's heart. "Yo Snake," Cruz says. "I knew that there was something wrong with dis nigga. Who are you, punk?"

"Yo man," Beast says calmly. "Put your guns down. I said that I used to be one of the Majestics. They shot my little bro and my mom in a drive-by last year. I ran to Miami to escape. They don't know that I'm back. They think I'm dead."

Snake, GI, and Cruz put their guns away.

"Snake," GI says. "I believe him. He wouldn't be selling us any guns if he were one of 'em."

"True dat," Cruz confirms.

"Ight then," Snake says. "Then what you want with us? Why do they Majestics think you are dead? You better start making some sense or you will be a dead nigga for sure."

"Ight then," Beast answers. "Just cool out. I was with my mom and my little brother when they were shot and killed. We were at the corner store. You know the 7-Eleven over on Fifth and Seventh? The Majestics did a drive-by. I don't know who they were after. I was on my phone and had my back turned. I took a bullet in the leg and went down. I rolled over to see who it was, and it was dem. Then I rolled over to my other side and saw my mom and little brother dead. Both had bullets in their heads and backs and were lying in their blood.

"I heard about your war with them. I want in. I wanna help. The next day after they killed my mom and bro, they gave me a death threat. They said that if I tell 5-0, they will kill the rest of my family. I sold weed to buy a ticket to go to Miami. I came back because I heard that Super Destroyers are at war with them. So I want in. I hate niggas so much."

"Why did they do that to your family?" Snake asked.

"They accused my cousin of selling one of them some bad coke. Said that it was spiked with something that killed him. So they started to come after my family. Bro, I will do whatever it takes to get in the Super Destroyers. Them niggas are increasing their members. I can get you into their hideout. I want to avenge my mamma and little bro. He was only ten years old. Now you know why I am here. I want in now."

"Ight. You want in?" Snake asks. "You gotta prove yourself worthy to be one of us. We have codes that we live by. We have codes for drive byes. We have a code if 5-0 comes."

"I heard about your codes," Beast says. "The Sun Rotates is when you are about to do a drive-by. The Clouds Come Down is when someone is doing a drive-by. Golden Sword is the code for cops in the area."

"How do you know our codes?" Snake asks.

"Did you know that I was friends with your boy T-Pot? He was like a little brother to me. His mom and my mom worked together doing some customer service job. She came over my house one night and brung him with her. T-Pot and I also have a friend in common. This friend was told to call me if anything happened to T-Pot. I got the call two nights before I met you guys. Then I got me a plane ticket."

"You got a phat car over there. You know how to drive that thing?" Snake asks.

"Step aside, nigga," Beast answers.

Beast gets back into his car. He starts the engine and revs the engine a few times. He then shifts the car into first gear and pops the clutch. The back tires of the Mustang spin, causing dirt and gravel to spit up from the bottom of the back wheels. The car takes off like a rocket. Beast speeds down the street. He goes to the corner and does a spinning U-turn into a 180-degree turnaround. Beast steps on the gas pedal until it touches the floor. The car takes off like a rocket and drives up the street. Beast drives to the end of the street, shifting very fast. The car goes top speed. When Beast gets to the end of the street, he does another spinning U-turn and drives back to Snake's house. He comes to a skidding stop just short of hitting a trash can. He gets out of the car, slams the door, then walks up to Snake.

"Does that answer your question, nigga?" Beast asks.

"Yo man," Cruz said. "Dis nigga knows how to drive. Where you learn dat?"

"My mama," Beast answers. "Now what do I do to get in?"

"Give me a minute to think about it," Snake says. "From what I just seen and heard about you, I gotta come up with something special just for you."

Beast walks over to the trunk of his car. He puts the key in the key hole and opens up the trunk. Snake, GI, and Cruz walk over to see what is in the trunk. The trunk is full of all kinds of guns and ammo. They all see AK-47's, M16s, hand grenades, and an M60.

"Snake," Beast says, "all these guns and ammo will be yours if you let me in."

"Ight then," Snake says. "Now you gotta pass my test. I see your M-60. You know how to use it?"

"Hell yeah," Beast answers. "I learned from my uncle in Miami. He was in Afghanistan fighting the Taliban. He was in Special Forces, Navy SEALS. He would always take me into the Everglades to teach me. He is afraid that ISIS would come after me. I had these guns in my storage space in LA."

Snake picks up the M-60 to take a closer look at it. "Man," he says, "5 – 0 makes me sick. Here's what I want you to do. If you are serious about becoming a Super Destroyer, then dis is your test." Snake gives out his assignment. After he tells Beast, Cruz gives Snake his cell phone. Snake dials a phone number.

"Yo nigga," Snake says. "I need you now. Yeah, you and Centipede. I got a job for both y'all niggas. Yeah, come over now. It's important. Okay, I'm over at GI's crib. Where you at? Ight, just come over now." Snake disconnects the call.

Ten minutes later, Toad and Centipede are at Snake's house. Snake gives out his plan. Toad, Centipede, and Beast take some hand grenades and a few extra guns along with the M-60 and bulletproof vests and soldier helmets. They get into Toad's car and drive off.

Toad drives to a nearby shopping mall. They drive around the parking lot for a few minutes. They spot a maroon-colored Mustang GT with a silver bottom half. Toad pulls into the parking space next to it. They all get out of Toad's car. They put on soldier helmets, ski masks, gloves, and bulletproof vests. Beast takes Toad's Slim Jim, slides it through the bottom of the Mustang's window, and pops open the lock. They unlock the doors. They take the weapons and put them in the Mustang. Toad and Centipede get into the car with Beast driving.

They drive off. Beast drives for a few miles. After a few minutes, the passenger side of the car is facing a police substation. Beast pulls the car over to the side of the road. They all get out. They pull out their guns. Then with a deep voice, Toad shouts, "THE SUN ROTATES!"

Beast, Toad, and Centipede open fire on the police substation. The bullets go everywhere. Police officers are getting shot and killed. The windows of the station are getting shattered. Police cars are getting blown up as Centipede and Toad are throwing hand grenades. Beast is using the M60 while Toad and Centipede are using AK-47s.

The police station is getting destroyed while other police officers are shot and killed. Some are trying to shoot back but ended up getting shot. After about three minutes, Toad throws two red smoke grenades. Beast, Toad, and Centipede get into the Mustang and drive off as the back tires spin and the bottom of the back tires spit up dirt and gravel.

Three dozen police officers are either wounded or killed. A one-story building was completely destroyed by gunfire and grenades. Ambulances and paramedics are all over the place. Many police officers are screaming in agony, and some are dying. Ten police officers are already dead. Beast drives the stolen Mustang back to where he stole it from at the shopping mall. He puts it back in the same spot. The three guys get out of the Mustang with their weapons. They put it in Toad's trunk. They take off their tactical gear. They get into Toad's car and drive back to Snake's house.

Chapter 6

Back at Snake's house, Snake turns on the evening news. On the TV screen, there is a white lady with shoulder-length dark hair holding a microphone. She is dressed in a red business dress, a white shirt under her jacket, and red high-heeled shoes. She is at the police station that has just been destroyed by Beast, Toad, and Centipede.

"This is Julie Stine reporting live from…" she mentions the police substation.

"Just moments ago, what once looked like a police substation is now turned to a war-torn destroyed building. Just minutes ago, a maroon-colored Mustang GT pulled up, and three people with black ski masks and tactical clothing got out and shot up this station using automatic weapons and hand grenades. About three dozen police officers were wounded or killed. We do have a report of ten police officers who were killed. Could this be an act of ISIS or Black Lives Matter?"

"YEAH!" Snake shouts with joy. He looks over at Beast who was sitting in the corner of the room. "Nigga, you are in man! You are in! Welcome to the family!"

"Yeah!" Toad shouts. "Party for him tonight!"

"You got that straight," Snake answers.

"Never before," the news reporter on the TV said, "in the history of any police department has anything like this ever happened. Right beside me is Sergeant Richard Butler. Sergeant Butler, what is the meaning of all this? What can you tell us about this?"

"It's hard to say. This is the kind of stuff that you would see in the movies like *Terminator*. Why this happened, I really don't know," Sergeant Butler answered.

"Has anyone been able to get the license plate number of the Mustang?" Julie asks.

"By the grace of God, somebody was able to see the plate number."

"Can you tell us what that number is or is that for the police department only?"

"This is for everybody to know. Be on the lookout for a maroon-colored Ford Mustang GT with license plate number VJ7 105. If you see this car, please do not approach the suspects in the car. They are very armed and extremely dangerous. If you see this car, please call 911. I repeat, do not approach the suspects."

The license plate number is on the screen.

"How exactly did this happen?" Julie asks.

"The Mustang came from the east block of Second Avenue. It got about midway and opened fire on us. I drew my pistol and began to fire back. The Lord Jesus was for sure on my side. When they saw me shooting back, they shot in my direction, missing me by less than an inch with an M60. I just had enough time to jump, dive, and roll and get behind those cement steps to avoid being shot. While I was lying on the ground, I reloaded my gun and returned fire. Then it was all over. The gunmen threw some red smoke grenades and took off in a cloud of smoke. I fought in Iraq in the streets of Bagdad. But I never thought I would be fighting terrorism right here in the United States where I work. This only goes to show that time is short. Jesus Christ is coming back soon."

"Thank you, Sergeant Butler. Now back to you, Jan, at the studio," Julie Stine concludes her interview.

"Well, good Lord!" Pastor Blanchard says as he picked up the remote to turn off the TV. "In all my years of ministry, I have never seen anything like this." Pastor Blanchard is with his wife at home.

Lynn gets up to wash the dishes that are left over from dinner.

"You know, dear," she says, "I think we should have a special prayer for those police officers and their families on Wednesday evening service."

"You are right about that. We should. I should go visit with some of them. I always admired them boys. Them thugs that shot up that police station are really gonna pay. They probably got more demons in them than hell itself. What would ever cause anyone to ever do that unless it's ISIS. I happen to know Sergeant Butler. He is a deacon over at Grace Gospel Tabernacle. I speak to him every time I go to his church to preach. He and I became good friends."

"Oh yes. He is such a blessing to us, David. Why don't you go see him tomorrow?"

"I think I will do just that."

Back at Snake's house, the news is still on. On the TV, there is a white man with a bald head. He is sitting behind a counter, and he gives the sports update.

"In the sports world, on Sunday, the Las Vegas Raiders defeated the Denver Broncos in a 37 – 34 come-from-behind victory in Denver. Let's go to Paul Allisson who is in Denver's Stadium."

"Raiders won too! That makes my day even better," GI says.

"Since when are you into football?" Cruz asks.

"I played some while I was in jail."

"He had to," Snake says. "He had to find some way to get away from Bubba when he was in the shower."

The rest of the guys were laughing at GI.

"Yo man," GI says. "Look who was forced to wear a dress in prison!"

The rest of the gang keep laughing.

"Well, at least we can avenge T-Pot's death," GI says.

"Man," Snake says. "I never really cared about that little nigga. It was always you and him who were best friends."

"Man," GI says. "What the hell you mean me and him? You were there for him too, nigga. You always said that you cared about him like a brother."

"Well, I lied, nigga."

"Man, I had enough of this," GI says. He gets up and walks out the house. He is shocked from what Snake has just said.

That is how Snake is. Whenever someone close to him dies, he always pushes the hurting and heartache inside. He will always say that he never cares about that person in order to forget that person.

He will turn the hurt into hate and anger towards that person. Then he would smoke weed to block out the rest of his emotions.

GI steps on the front porch and walks down the steps. He walks towards his house.

"Hey, GI," a girl's voice says in a distance. He turns and sees Kristal standing on the porch just two houses down from Shake's house. She is hanging out with a girl from church. When he sees them, he just keeps walking to his house. But Kristal keeps calling out to him. She and her friend run to him. GI sits on the front step of his house.

"Hey, GI," Kristal says. "What's the matter? Are you okay?"

"Yeah," GI says. "I'm ight. Who's this honey wit' you?"

"This is Bee Bee. Her dad is an usher at our church."

"What she doing here?"

"She lives over there. I was just hanging out with her today. What you doing?"

"I was just thinking about some stuff," he answers. "Snake cussed me out saying that he never cared about T-Pot."

"Oh, he's just lying," Kristal says. "That's just Snake being a snake. Did you hear on the news about the police station being shot up?"

"Yeah. They think it's ISIS attacking them."

While Kristal is talking, he begins to have a flashback from that tall bald-headed black man preaching about the gang lifestyle.

Is it really worth it? Is it really worth getting shot up so that your homeboy could continue his drug dealing? the man in his flashback is saying. *You get shot up, rotting your poor soul in hell. Then you are forgotten here on earth forever. The person who shot you has no guilt or remorse about what he did to you. He don't give a hoot about your soul.*

"GI?" Kristal asks. "Are you okay?"

He comes out of his flashback. He breathes a big puff of air and shakes his head.

"What's the matter?" Kristal asks.

"Nothing," he says. "Just remembering something when I was in jail."

"What were you thinking about? You look troubled by something. Are you? I think it's this gang thing."

When she says that, he puts his face in his hands.

"Don't you think that it is time to get out? Do you value your life?" Kristal asks softly.

"I can't get out," GI says.

"Why?"

"Because I feel like they are the only family I got. I feel like I can't get out because I feel like I belong to them. Snake and I run the gang together. The gang owns my soul."

"You can accept Jesus," Bee Bee says. "Then Jesus can own your soul."

"I don't want Jesus to own my soul. How can anybody who I can't see own anything?"

"The Bible says that we walk by faith and not by sight. But Jesus Christ said, 'Blessed are they who believe and not see.' So don't worry if you can't see Jesus. He's not always gonna appear to everyone, except on the day he returns to take his church home. All you have to do is confess with your mouth and believe with your heart that God raised Jesus from the grave, and you will be saved."

"Bee Bee, I don't think that it's my time to get saved yet. What the hell am I getting saved from anyway?"

"From hell," Kristal says. "From bondages. From damnation of your soul. You can have liberty in Jesus Christ. You can have peace and joy in life. You can have everlasting life. Unless you want to live eternally in the lake of fire. That is where you will burn forever if you don't get saved."

"Well, it's like I said. It's not my time yet."

"That's the problem that we all face," Kristal says. "We die before our time. The last thing that cop said on TV was, 'Jesus is coming back again.' We need to get ready. Where do you think T-Pot is right now?"

"Yo," GI says. "Step off T-Pot! Leave him out of this. You told him that he was better off dead by being in the gang. You don't care about him either! And you come here preaching about getting 'saved' and 'everlasting life,' and all that kind of shi…"

"I never said that to him!" Kristal shouts.

"He told me you did. You calling him a liar?"

"Look, GI. I said to him, 'You are better off dead for Christ than being in this gang.' Ask Bee Bee. She's my witness."

"She's telling you the truth, GI," Bee Bee said. "I was right there. Jackie was with us that night. The three of us ran into him at BK."

"Man," GI says. "Y'all lying!"

"No," Kristal says. "I swear with God as my final witness. It happened while you were in jail. Jackie, Bee Bee, and I went to a BK after church. We tried to help him. I'm sorry he had to die like that. But if you live by the sword, you will also die by the sword. Matthew 26:52."

Kristal is in tears.

"Ight then. I believe you. You and T-Pot would have made a good couple. I saw the nigga who shot him. I saw him walk away. But nobody saw who shot Jackie."

"So what are you gonna do now?" Kristal asks.

"I know what I feel like doing."

"But what are you gonna do?"

"I don't know." GI shrugs his shoulders.

"Why don't you come down to our church? If you are not busy, come down tonight. I got my mom's car."

He then hears a voice in his head saying, *Go. Go to church now.*

Then he heard another voice in his head saying, *Celebrate the arrival of the Beast.*

"I got a party to go to tonight," he answers. "Maybe I will go on a Sunday."

That night, the gang is at Snake's house. They have everything going on to give Beast a party. They all have alcohol, weed, chips, soda, and a prostitute for Beast. Dragon is the lookout for the night. Flicker is the DJ for the party. He sets up all his equipment in the corner of the living room. Later that evening, Snake's front door opens up, and two dozen prostitutes come into the house.

"Money for your honey! Honies in the house!" Flicker announces into the microphone.

Flicker switches the CD into some slow music. Every guy has a girl dancing with them. Snake and Toad have two. Everyone is smoking dope and drinking alcohol. GI is the only one who is not smoking anything. By midnight, every guy has sex with a prostitute. They all take turns using Snake's bedroom. GI is one of the first ones because of his mother's curfew.

The next morning, the gang is all hung over and passed out on the floor at Snake's house. Snake is in his room sleeping. All the prostitutes are gone. GI does not wake up until twelve thirty in the afternoon. It's a Saturday afternoon, and it's a sunny day. It's the third day of November.

When GI wakes up, he gets on the phone and calls Kristal.

"Yo, what's up, baby?" GI asks when Kristal answers the phone.

"Hey, GI," she says.

"What you doing tonight?" he asks.

"I am a little busy tonight. What you doing tomorrow morning?"

"I wanna spend it with you."

She thought for a minute. "Okay. How does ten thirty tomorrow morning sound to you?"

"What do you wanna do? Your place or mine?"

"I'll pick you up at your house at ten thirty, and we will go out. Write it down now."

"Ight. I'll write it down, and I'll be ready for you."

GI has no idea of what Kristal is planning to do with him. He goes to his clock radio and sets his alarm for nine thirty the next morning. He thinks that he is going on an early morning date with Kristal tomorrow. After he sets his alarm, he takes a shower. Later on that day, he meets with his probation officer for his weekly appointment.

"Well, Rubin, how have you been this week?" Probation Officer Sean Walker asks.

"I been doing ight," GI says.

"Talk to me in English. I don't understand this 'ight' nonsense."

"Well, I don't smoke weed anymore."

"Tell me what you have been doing this week. Are things working out between you and your mother?"

"Yeah. Things are working out straight."

"Have you been in church yet?"

"Nope. Don't plan to."

"Why?"

"Cause I ain't got no reason to go."

"How about you visit my church?"

"What church is that?"

"Grace Gospel Tabernacle. Did you see the interview with the cop on the news?"

"Which one?"

"Sergeant Richard Butler. They interviewed him when that police station was destroyed by all that gunfire."

"Yeah. I seen him. So what?"

"Well, I think you should go to church. In fact, I recommend Holy Revival Ministries. It's not such a far walk for you. Go there tomorrow."

"I'm busy tomorrow. I got a date."

"I'm not going to make you break your date. But I think that going to church will do wonders for you. I can't force you. I can only encourage you to go. Jesus Christ is the only way out of what you got yourself into."

"Yeah, whatever. I don't believe in him. Jesus was just another black prophet who was sent by God to condemn the people of Israel."

"You ever read John 3:16?"

"No. Why?"

"For your assignment, I want you to look up John 3:16. I want you to have it memorized by next week. The book of John is a great book of the Bible. It is right before the book of Acts. I am going to give you a small Bible."

Sean opens the top right drawer of his desk. He reaches in and takes out a small pocket-size Bible and hands it to GI.

"Here is the New Testament only. This is the NIV, New International Version. You don't have to read it now. But you do have to have John 3:16 memorized by next week. Thanks for coming in today. You forgot last week's appointment, but I let it slide. I won't next time. You better be here same time."

Sean hands GI a small plastic cup with a plastic lid. "Don't forget to fill this cup on your way out. You better be clean."

"Ight. I'll see you next week. I'll fill up this cup and try not to drink it."

The next morning, GI wakes up to his music blasting from his alarm clock radio. At ten thirty, he is dressed up and ready to go out with Kristal. She arrives at 10:32 a.m.

Kristal has her mom's old white four-door Ford Focus. Bee Bee is in the front passenger seat. Both girls are excited to see GI. He gets into the back seat.

"Yo wat up, Kris? Wat up, Bee? Who car is dis?" GI asks.

"Hey, G. How you been? This is my mom's car. She let me use it to pick you up," Kristal says.

Rubin sees a Bible in the back seat. He just figures that since Kristal is a Christian that she just left it there. Suddenly, a voice went off in his head, *John 3:16.* But he ignores it. Kristal drives off down the street. A few minutes later, she drives into the parking lot of Holy Revival Ministries.

"Hey, what we doing here?" GI asks.

"Don't worry about it. You'll see," Kristal says.

"What will I see?"

"There's gonna be a lot of action going on here this morning. I'm talking about nonstop action. Then we can go out after," Kristal says with excitement.

"Just watch and see," Bee Bee says.

Kristal parks the car, and everybody gets out. They go into the church. They sit in the middle of the fourth row. Rubin is wearing black jeans and an LA Lakers T-shirt with white high-top sneakers.

The choir set themselves up onstage. The worship singers test the mics for sound checks. They arrange themselves into their right places. The church band checks their instruments. Anthony Johnson grabs the main mic. He goes to the front of the stage where the podium is. He watches the church fill up with people. The church is now about 85 to 90 percent full. Anthony speaks into the mic.

"Let's get it on!" he shouts. The choir, band, and worship singers suddenly start singing "I Will Celebrate." Anthony leads the church like he does every Sunday as the worship leader. The worship goes on for about forty-five minutes. When Pastor David Blanchard comes on the stage, he takes the lead in worship to the song "Let It Rain."

Everyone is standing with their hands in the air and worshiping. Rubin is the only one who is sitting down. He is sitting with his arms crossed over his chest. His feet are under the pew that is in front of him. After the song is over, Pastor David speaks into the mic.

"Well, go ahead and praise him! Praise him all day! Praise him all night. Praise him forever. When the praises go up, his blessings come down! Give God the glory! Give him thanks and praise! Give him all the honor! It is Jesus Christ who is setting you free!"

The whole church is going crazy. They are shouting their victories. But they are shouting unto the Lord.

"Hallelujah! Praise the Lord!" Pastor David starts to speak in a language that nobody understands. Then he begins to pray.

"Father God, we come to you in the name of your Son Jesus Christ. We ask that you would fill this place with the power of the Holy Spirit. I ask that you would reach down and touch somebody who really needs a touch from above. I ask that you would save somebody. I ask that this message that I am about to preach would penetrate the hearts and minds of your people here today. I ask that seeds will be planted. Let deliverance go forth in this church today. I ask that you would give everybody that is here today an ear to hear what the spirit is saying to the church. Yes, my Lord God, Jehovah, who is the creator of the universe. I pray in the name of Jesus Christ. Amen. And the church said?"

"Amen," the church said together in unison.

"Well, God is a good God and his mercies endures forever. Before you are seated, turn around and hug somebody. Tell them, 'If it had not been for me, you would be the best-looking person in the world.' Praise God."

Everybody does what Pastor Blanchard said, and a lot of joyful laughs break out of many people. Everyone walks around inside the church, greeting each other. After a few minutes, they are all back in their seats sitting down.

"When I said 'me,' I meant, me, Pastor David Blanchard," he says jokingly. Everybody is laughing at him.

"Do we have any first-time visitors? Would you please stand up?"

About ten people stand up. GI sits down. He is still sitting with his arms folded across his chest and his feet are under the pew in front of him. He just do not want to budge.

All the first-time visitors are given a newsletter about the church, as well as an information about a card to fill out. They are all greeted with a round of applause from everybody else.

Pastor David goes on speaking. "Welcome to Holy Revival Ministries. I am Pastor David Blanchard. Those who are first-time visitors are also welcomed back to our Sunday night service at seven thirty in the evening. I will be preaching about the power of praise and worship. Worship is something that we take seriously in this church. You don't want to miss this message. It will be a power-packed message with some praise and worship. Amen.

"This morning's message is entitled, 'Two Roads.' Turn with me in your Bibles to the Gospel of Matthew chapter 7." He waits for everyone to get to Matthew 7. Then he goes on speaking. "From verse 13, we read the words of Jesus saying, 'Enter ye in at the straight gate; for wide is the gate, and broad is the way that leadeth to destruction, and many there go in threat. Because straight is the gate and narrow is the way, which leadeth unto life, and a few find it.' The NIV says, 'Broad is the road that leads to destruction.' And 'Narrow is the road that leads to life.'

"God told me to preach this message because some of you are on that road to destruction. But I am here to give you a message of hope. That's why Jesus said in John 3:16–17, 'For God so loved the world that He gave His only begotten Son, that whosoever believeth in Him should not perish, but have everlasting life. For God sent not His Son into the world to condemn the world; but that through Him might be Saved.'

"God did not send Jesus to condemn you. No! God sent Jesus to save you! Some of you are on that road to destruction. But Jesus can give you everlasting life so that you don't have to go down that road that leads to destruction."

By this time, GI sits up. He suddenly begins to listen. Pastor David goes on. He walks down the steps that are in front of the stage. He goes to the altar. He turns his body so that he is facing south.

"Jesus speaks about two roads, one that leads to life and one that leads to destruction. Let's say that right in front of me is the road that leads to destruction. Some of you are walking down this road right now and don't realize what you are getting into. Some of you don't see where you are going. Hell is straight ahead, and you don't even know it. You don't know where this road leads to or how much worse things are gonna get."

Pastor David starts to walk forward to the south. He walks slowly.

"Birds head south in the winter and go back north after the spring. But when you go south of heaven, you go straight to hell. When you get to hell, you can't ever go north unless you turn around before you get there and do a 180-degree turn towards Jesus. But on that road to destruction, you don't know what your final destination is until you get there. Some of you know what your destination is and don't care."

Pastor David turns around. He starts to walk north. He continues to walk slowly up the altar.

"The other road that Jesus spoke about is the road that leads to life. It's a straight and narrow road that leads to life. You know where it leads to! You know that it leads to life. It is the road that you want to be on. It's the road that leads you to salvation! You can see Jesus Christ standing at the end of the road with his arms stretched out to you at the end of the road! Can I get a witness in here?!"

Some people were standing up and shouting.

"Somebody help me in here! This is the road to everlasting life! Are you on it?!"

Pastor David turns around and starts to walk south again.

"Do you see what I just did? I just turned around. I turned my back on Jesus. Every time you walk down this road that leads to destruction, you turn your back on Jesus. You are saying no to salvation. You are saying, 'No, I don't want salvation.' You are saying, 'No, I don't want to go to heaven.' I often hear people say that no means no! Be sure that you know what you are saying no to." He faces the people.

"A girl goes on a date. She tells the guy that she doesn't want to be touched in certain areas of her body. They go up on some high cliff in his car. They go to some lover's point or something like that. They begin to make out in the back seat. He touches her breasts and the girl says no. He touches her breasts again. She says no again. Then she slaps him in the face and asks him to take her home. Right there, no means no. I understand that. That is when no should mean no.

"Let's say that you are at your job. You have another two or three hours to go, and you realize that your favorite TV show will be on soon. You know that a certain character is gonna have a baby or might get shot and killed. Or that person in your favorite TV show is getting married.

"I know how some of you sisters are so into weddings. You don't care how much you hate that TV show. If there's a wedding on that show, you will watch it. Some of you will even call out sick at your jobs just to watch that show. As the pastor of this church, I enjoy marrying couples. But I am not obsessed with watching weddings on TV. I don't care what the show is.

"So there you are at your job and then, suddenly, you remember that your favorite character on your favorite TV show is getting married. You beg and plead with your boss to let you go home early. You even tell your bosses excuses why you want to go home. Your boss tells you no. You keep begging and he still says no.

"My wife had the same experience with this, and so did some of you. I remember hearing some stories about it. Don't come to me anymore about it. Because when your boss says, no, then no means no! Stop coming to me about it. I will take your boss' side. Unless it is a family emergency. That is a different situation.

"Some of you even told me, 'Oh, but I am a child of the king of kings. I shouldn't have to listen to him. He's not even a Christian.' Do you want a paycheck every week? Then listen to him!"

A few people said, "Amen." Some laughed.

"I understand that no means no. But what I don't understand about no meaning no is when you say no to Jesus Christ and His gift of salvation. That is what you do when you say no to Jesus. You choose to walk down the road of destruction when you say no to Jesus. Does your life mean anything to you? Do you realize what John 3:16 is all about? Anyone who believes in what Jesus did will have freedom and everlasting life."

Pastor David walks back up the steps of the altar. Slow music begins to play.

"God will welcome you into his kingdom if you would only repent of your sins. Stop and get out of that sin that you are in. Stop walking down that road of destruction and turn around to walk on that road that leads to eternal life. My friends, walking down that road that leads to destruction is like walking the plank on a pirate ship. Some of you might remember some of the old pirate movies. What would happen if you had to walk the plank? You fall into the ocean. There are sharks in the ocean that would just love to have you for a meal. And you will get eaten alive.

"When you turn around and walk road that leads to life, it's like walking on streets of gold. When you get to the end, you are entering into your mansion. Which road would you rather be walking on?

"Everybody bow your heads and close your eyes. I know that what I just preached about has just woken some of you up. I know that some of you felt a touch from above in your hearts. Jesus wants to save you. Some of you are saying, 'Man, my life is a mess.' Or, 'I can't get out of the mess that I am in. But if this Jesus can get me out, then I will serve him for the rest of my life.' And some of you are saying to yourselves, 'You know what, this preacher is right. I've been walking down that road that leads to destruction for too long.' Only you know what that road is that you are walking down on. Maybe it's crack cocaine. Maybe it's prostitution. Maybe it's the gang lifestyle and you feel like you can't get out.

"You can choose the road that leads to life which is in Jesus Christ, or you can choose to walk down the road that leads to destruction which is eternal death. The plank. The choice is yours.

How many people want to choose the road that leads to eternal life that only comes through Jesus Christ? Then put your hands up."

A whole lot of hands are raised in the air.

"Yes. I see those hands. I can see the hands in the back rows. Not just me. Jesus sees your hand. You are so precious in his sight. Anymore?"

A few more hands go up. GI's hands stay down and are still folded across his chest. Everybody has their heads bowed and their eyes closed except for the ones who have their hands raised. Some of them are in tears.

"Now that you have raised your hands, I want you to stand up. Oh praise the Lord in here!"

Everyone who is sitting is giving the people applause. GI is not moving at all. He just does not care.

"The next thing that I want you to do is come and meet me at this altar. Come right now. There is plenty of room at the altar."

The ones who have raised their hands get out of their seats and walk down the isle of the church. About thirty people walk to the altar. Some are from gangs. Some are crackheads. Some girls are prostitutes. While they are at the altar, some of the elders of the church are standing behind them, directing others where to go. After about ten minutes, people stop coming to the altar. GI sits in his seat.

"Well, praise the Lord in here. God is so awesome! All of you are so special to God. Are you ready to accept Jesus into your hearts?"

Some nod. Some say yes, and some say nothing.

"I congratulate you for making the most important decision of your lives. Now, I want you to repeat this prayer after me. Say this to Jesus with all your heart, 'Lord Jesus, I come to you now. Just as I am, I come. I ask that you would forgive me of all my sins. Wash me and cleanse me with your Blood. Lord Jesus, I ask you to come into my heart and be my Lord and Savior. From this day forward, I am yours and you are mine. Thank you, Lord, for saving me. In the name of Jesus, I pray. Amen."

Every word of this prayer is repeated line by line by everyone at the altar.

"Go ahead and put your hands together for these people."

Everyone else is giving them a standing ovation. Some are shouting and some are whistling.

"The Bible says, 'You are a new creation in Christ.' The worst is over, and the best is yet to come. Now, I would like for you to go with these counselors into this room. Follow this man right here. Raise your hand, Brother Wilson."

They all go with Brother Wilson into the choir room to be ministered by Brother Wilson and other counselors. Pastor David closes the service by collecting the tithes and offerings. Then he prays a closing prayer and dismisses everybody, and the service was over.

Chapter 7

Everybody is walking out of the church doors. GI and Kristal are already outside the church. Bee Bee stays in.

"Yo, what you bring me here for?" Rubin asks Kristal.

"The Bible says, 'Do the work of an evangelist.' So I invited you to church. That's why."

"Man, you lie. You didn't bring me here for dat."

"I also wanted you to meet someone."

"Who?"

"A friend. Just wait a few minutes. He's downstairs getting done with teaching Sunday school with the little kids."

"Sunday school? Man you want me to meet some weak Sunday school teacher? He's probably some gay fag wanting to feel me up all over telling me that he loves me."

"Will you calm down, GI? You don't even know who this person that I want you to meet yet. But I'm sure he will love you."

Bee Bee walks out. She is holding hands with a tall black man. The man is six foot three. He works out regularly at the gym. He is the size of an NFL linebacker. He is wearing a white-colored suit with a black tie and a light-blue dress shirt under his dress jacket. He has a slightly bald head with only a bit of peach fuzz on top. They walk over to where Kristal and GI are talking. Kristal greets the man with a big hug. GI looks at the man in disbelief.

"No way, man!" GI says. "It can't be!"

"Rubin," Kristal said, "this is the man that I wanted you to meet. Do you remember Bruce Sanders? He was also known as Junkblood, former Super Destroyer."

"How ya doing, GI? Praise the Lord! Good to see ya again," Bruce says excitedly.

GI gives Bruce a big hug.

"My God!" GI says. "I thought you were dead!"

"What?" Bruce asks.

"Nigga, I thought you were dead, man."

"How could you think that?"

"T-Pot told me that you ODed on that junk that you kept put-ting in your veins."

"Brother, I've been clean and sober for about two years. It's all about Jesus. They used to call me *Junkblood*, but now, I got a taste of the *real blood*. That's the only drug that I am taking. Nothing but the blood of Jesus!"

"Nigga, why the sudden change? You going with Bee Bee?"

"Yeah. We been together for six months now. She is my beau-tiful baby. She's my double B. After six months, I can now say that. She's my most-prized possession." Bruce puts his arms around her and says, "One day, she will be my beautiful bride."

Bee Bee lets out a breath of fresh air and melts in his arms.

"Hey yo," GI says. "You never answered my question. Why did you leave the Destroyers?"

"Hey, bro. What are your plans right now?"

"I don't know. You wanna chill out a while?"

"Yeah. Over at BK right now."

"Ight bro. Let's go."

They get into Kristal's car and drive to Burger King. When they get there, they go inside, order their lunch, and sit down at a booth.

"Man," GI says. "I can't get over it. You were a ninety-five-pound heroin junkie gangsta. Now you are, what, two-hundred-something-pound Sunday school teacher?"

"GI," Bruce said. "I got a new change in my life. Before, I was putting about two hundred dollars of heroin a day into my veins. The last time you saw me, I was so messed up on that junk, and I weighed just over a hundred pounds. I was just all skin and bones and dying.

"GI, the reason that I was doing all that was because I was hurt-ing. I was hurting from my family. I was abused from childhood by my family. You know about most of my life growing up. I saw abuse my whole life growing up. I then saw drugs enter my family through my dad, and it spread like a wildfire. My dad died of an overdose of heroin and alcohol at the same time. He downed a bottle of rum and took too much mix of heroin and cocaine and speed. I saw him shoot all that shi'. Excuse me. That junk into his arm right in front of me. Before he did that, he said that I should continue the family tradition and do heroin till I die.

"The next year, I saw my mom put a .38 to her head and blow her brains out. I was only twelve years old. Then I met your cousin. My older brother had later on had been arrested for murder. He is on death row in San Quinton right now. He killed three people in first-degree murder, one of which was a cop. That's when I met Snake. He had already started the Super Destroyers with you, and I joined.

"I felt like I had nowhere else to go. Snake and you made me feel acceptance like family. I felt a false sense of security, like I belonged there. Then Lizard and Scorpion would always hook me up with what I thought was the best drug in the world, heroin.

"I remember the night you were arrested. That week, my brother was also arrested. That's when my life began to change. My cousin Brian was an LA Crip. I then saw him get shot and killed in a drive-by from a Blood. That woke me up. After we had the funeral, the next day, I went over to Long Beach and hung out at the shipyard to do some thinking. I still had an addiction to heroin, and I felt like I couldn't quit. But on that day I went to the shipyard, I did not have any urge to do any drugs at all. I didn't even realize it. I just sat on a pile of pallets overlooking the water.

"Then out of nowhere, I heard someone yell out, 'John 3:16!' Right under the pallet that I was sitting on was one of those pocket-size Bibles. I didn't know how it got there. It was the New Testament in the NIV. I picked it up. I tried to burn it, but my lighter would not work. It would only give off sparks. I tried to throw the Bible into the water. But every time I tried, my elbow would suddenly get some bad pain. You know the pain that pitchers in baseball get? The pain got worse every time I tried to raise my arm to throw the Bible into the water.

"Then I heard another voice saying, 'John 3:16.' I just did not know what was going on. I just bawled out crying. Then out of nowhere, a man in a white suit stood next to me. I just felt an overwhelming feeling of peace all around me. The man said to me, 'Give it up, brother. The Lord wants you.' I looked at the ocean. When I turned to look at the man, he was gone! He was nowhere to be found! I didn't want to, but I read John 3:16.

"I was amazed when I read it. I didn't understand how God could send His Son to die for us. I had no idea that I could be saved through Jesus Christ. I then turned to Matthew 11, and I read verses 28 through 30. Jesus wants us to come to him, and he will give us rest. I started to see my life. I saw all the abuse, the drugs, the suicide of my mother, my dad dying right in front of me. I saw the death of my cousin who I was close to. I saw my brother going to death row.

"I asked myself, *Where is my life going?* I turned over to Acts 16:31. The only thing that stuck out to me was, 'Believe in the Lord Jesus and you will be Saved.' Then I saw in Revelation 3:20, Jesus was saying, 'I stand at the door of your heart and knock. If anyone hears my voice and opens the door, I will come in.' From there through my tears, I prayed, 'Jesus, if You would take all the drugs, all the gangsta lifestyle and heal this hurting that I have in my life, then I will open the door of my heart and let you in.'

"When I prayed that prayer, a car pulled up and I heard some church music blasting from the car stereo. I then threw my lighter into the water. I also threw my 9mm into the water. I did not feel any pain or soreness in my elbow. I got up and walked over to the car to see who it was. It was a white man with blond hair. He was wearing a blue T-shirt with a pair of white shorts and sandals.

"He looked at me and called out to me, 'Hey brother! You need a ride to church?' I ran up to him and gave him a big hug. Next thing I know, I was in his red convertible sports car and he gave me a ride to Holy Revival Ministries. When he dropped me off, I wasn't even halfway to the church doors. I turned to look at the car to thank the driver, and he was gone. Car and all just disappeared. But from all the songs that he played in the car, only one line from a song stood out in my head. 'Lets us go into the house of the Lord.'

"When I went into the church, I met someone named William Johnson. Today, he is one of my best friends and mentors. God used him to minister to me. On that day, I totally gave my life over to Jesus Christ. I have been set free from drugs and healed from the abuse that I have been through growing up. I have had all kinds of demons cast out of me. I've been living a new clean life. That is why I left the gang. The church is an area where the Super Destroyers never go to. I live around the corner from the church."

"Man," GI says. "What an amazing story. T-Pot told me all this time dat you were dead of an OD. So that's why I thought you were dead."

"Well, he's right. I am dead."

"What? Nigga, you ain't dead. You crazy!" GI says, laughing.

"No. For real, G. I am dead. The Bible says that I am dead to this world but alive unto God. In other words, I am a new creation in Christ. The person you used to know, the old Bruce, has died. What you are looking at is a new creation in Christ."

"Well," GI says sadly. "T-Pot is dead also."

"Yeah. I heard."

"Why weren't you there at the picnic?"

"I was working on that day T-Pot got shot. Nobody ever told me about the funeral."

"Where are you working now?"

"In the mall."

"For real? Which store?"

"Bright Lights Bookstore. My uncle from Chicago moved here last year, and we opened up the store in the mall."

"You're a Sunday school teacher and a bookworm too?"

"It's a Christian bookstore. Did you see the Haitian usher at the back of the church? He was the first one who greeted you when you first came in. He gave you a hug."

"Yeah. Did you see me when I came in?"

"Yeah. I saw you when you came in. I was up front of the church. Then I had to go to work with the kids. Anyways, that is my uncle Peter. We are the owners of Bright Lights Bookstore. Come on in one time. We close at nine in the evening. I can hook you up with some cool stuff and music. We got some awesome Christian rap music. Ever heard of NF? You might like his music. It is a great place to work. We fill the place up with God's presence every day that we work. We are closed on Sundays."

"Why do you call it Bright Lights for?"

"Jesus said in Matthew 5:13, 'We are the Light of the world.' And a few verses later, it says, 'Let your Light shine before men.' So that's why we named our store Bright Lights Bookstore. It's been open for about a year. God has really blessed our business."

"Hey, man, why don't you come and visit Snake? I know you'll miss T-Pot forever."

"Yeah, you right. I will miss T-Pot. But then I'm not surprised. He was headed in that direction. I still find myself grieving over his death. Only if I tried a little harder, he wouldn't have gotten killed."

"Honey," Bee Bee says. "Don't blame yourself. You did what you could. He chose to walk down that road. He would have still gone to that picnic even if you had chained him to his bed."

"I warned him not to go," Bee Bee says. "He was so stubborn."

"Hey, GI," Bruce says. "I am sorry about your girl getting shot. I am also sorry about T-Pot. Are you getting tired of all this killing? I mean, who's next?"

"I'm not asking or telling you to quit the gang. I know that it is hard to leave all your homies. I know the feeling that it brings when you are with the boys. I know, bro. I've been there. But let me ask you, what's in it for you? What future does it have for you? Who will die next? I know you been thinking about it. It does seem hard to get out right now. But there is freedom from it. Is it really worth staying in it? Do you want to see another homie in another body bag from a bullet? Do you yourself wanna end up six feet under and forgotten forever?

"The person who kills you don't care about you or what he did. The only thing that he cares about is killing you first. It's all about kill or be killed. Kill your enemy before he has a chance to kill you and not even think about prison. I don't even know when my brother's execution date is. He is a man who is guilty of murder. He didn't care about anything when he pulled that trigger. His attitude was like, 'Prison? Who cares?' Now look where he is today."

"You saw T-Pot's death coming?"

"Yeah. I did. I see it coming to Snake also if he don't repent and change. Bro, God has brought us here today for a reason. The reason is for you to open your eyes. I know how much you want to get revenge. Especially for Jackie. I can see the anger in your eyes. I felt that way when my cousin was killed. I understand it. I know that you want revenge. You all do."

"Yeah, I'm gonna get even and avenge Jackie and T-Pot's death."

"Is it worth it?"

"Hell yeah, it's worth it. It will make me feel better."

"What if you get killed first?"

"Then at least I die knowing that I tried to avenge them. All I care about is avenging my people. We just got a new member."

"Oh yeah? Who's the man?"

"His name is Beast. You should meet him. Seems pretty cool."

"I'm not sure I want to meet him. At least, not right now. How's Toad doing? Is he still big?"

"Yeah. He still works out. How did you get so big? You weighed just over a hundred pounds. What happened?"

"I started working out after I got delivered from all that drugs that I was taking. I just worked out and ate right. When I was pumping that junk into my veins, I never ate anything. Every time I got hungry, instead of food, I chose the needle. There was more demons in those drugs than anything I have ever been through before."

"You got clean arms?"

"No, G. My arms still have small needle scabs. Some of them will never go away because I was such a heavy user. Now, I use these scars as testimonies of what God has delivered me from. I use these scars to tell young people about what I been through."

GI feels a buzz on his right hip bone. He looks down at his cell phone. He answers it. "Yo. What's up, bro?"

"What you doing, bro?" It is Cruz.

"What's up, nigga?"

"Where you at?"

"Over at BK."

"Which one?"

"Over on 20th street. What you want?"

"Snake says to meet us over at his house."

"Ight. Right now?"

"Yeah now."

"Ight cool. I be there soon."

They both hang up.

"Yo bro. I gotta jet. I'll walk home. See ya'll later. Junkblood, it was good to see you again. Come on by later. I'll tell Snake and the rest I seen ya."

"What you walking home for?" Kristal asks. "I'll drive you home."

"Na. That's ight. I can walk."

"You sure?" Bruce asks.

"Don't worry about me. I'm strapped. Got a .38 on me."

GI lifts up his T-shirt and shows his .38 and leaves.

*****

Rubin gets to Snake's house. Snake's mother opens the door.

"Oh hello, Rubin. Come on in, baby," Snake's mother says. "Jamal is in his room. He'll be right out. How's your momma?"

"My momma's ight."

"I haven't seen her in a while. I been working. Long hours. You want some fresh-made pie?"

"No thanks, Aunt Mona. I was over at BK for lunch. Can I go see Snake?"

"Sure, baby. Give your Aunt Mona a kiss."

He gives her a kiss on her cheek followed with a hug. He walks into Snake's room. He sees Snake dancing to some rap music.

"Yo wat up, nigga? You dancing like a fool!" GI says. "Wat you playin'? Where Cruz at?"

Snake waits for the song to end. He turns the radio off.

"You so funky, man," Snake says. "Cruz had to split. Dis DJ is new."

60

"Word?"

"Word straight. Station new too. Kick. It's kickin'. Like yo breath is kickin'."

"So what's up, cuz? What you need me over for?"

"What you doing over at BK?"

"I was chillin' with, guess who?"

"Who?"

"Junkblood."

"What? Nigga you lie. Dat nigga die long time ago."

"No. For real. He alive."

"T-Pot told me that he OD."

"Snake, T-Pot lie. Junkblood became a born-again Christian."

"Well, what do you know? Is he still skinny, all skin and bones?"

"Hell no! He a big nigga now. He about Toad's size. He go with this chick named Bee Bee."

"Well, Junkblood can come back anytime he wants to. If he decides to."

"Well, what's going on today? What's everyone up to?"

"They all coming here today. I finally got a way to get them Majestics. I got all the Destroyers coming over."

Ten minutes later, all of the Super Destroyers were over at Snake's house on the front lawn. Beast was sitting on the steps. Toad knocks at the door. Snake comes walking out with GI.

"Yo, what's up, homies?" Snake called out as he was walking out the door. "Congrats to the new nigga of the Super Destroyers. Dis nigga's gonna help us and hook us up. Right, homie?"

"You got that straight," answers Beast.

"I got a plan that will win the war. Beast can get us into their hideout. Tell us where it is, Beast."

Beast stands up. They all make a semicircle around him.

"Their hideout is an old abandoned building in South Central. It's over on South West 13th street. The building is still up. It's a four-story building and no elevator. They hang out all over the building. They have two armed lookouts with AK-47s. If you can get past them, you can get in. They also have grenades on them. They also have guards at the back doors of the building. They are easy to take out if you are smart."

"That's where you come in," Snake interrupts. "I got a real job for you"

Snake gives out his plan.

Chapter 8

After Snake gives his plan, GI's mother comes outside. She is wearing a bathrobe and curlers in her hair with a shower cap over the curlers.

"Yo, Rubin," Ginalee calls out. "You got a phone call on my landline."

"Hi, Aunt Gina!" Snake calls out.

"Oh hello, Jamal. How you doing, baby? Tell your momma I said hello. Tell her to call me later."

"Okay, Aunt Gina. She's home right now. Should I get her?" Snake asks.

"Thank you, baby. Tell her to come over."

"Rubin, I said get over here! Answer your call! Don't know why you keep getting calls on my landline. I told you that I don't want you getting any calls on my phone."

Snake goes in his house to get Monna. GI went to answer the phone. The rest of the gang wait outside in front of Snake's house. Snake comes out with his mother. Monna goes over to where Ginalee is and they start to talk.

Meanwhile, GI is on the phone.

"So, yo Junkblood," GI says. "Are you coming over later?"

"Maybe some other time. What are you guys doing later?"

"I don't know."

"Hey, GI. Have you given it any thought to what I was saying?"

"So are you saying that I should let the nigga who shot T-Pot and Jackie off the hook? Should I just let them run free?"

"Do you really wanna hold the pain of T-Pot and Jackie inside forever? Do you want to grieve their deaths forever? Even if you do get your revenge, it's still gonna be hard on you. It will be even worse.

63

"I don't know what kind of a plan that Snake has, but God always has a better plan than anyone else. God wants you to forgive. The Bible says, 'Vengeance is mine says the Lord.' I believe that justice should be done God's way."

GI thinks for a moment.

"How do I forgive someone for something like that?"

"The Bible says, 'Forgive seventy times seven.' Jesus said that. Hey, man, I know it's hard to forgive. But it takes more of a man to forgive than not to forgive at all. What do you wanna do? Do you wanna go down the road of destruction or on the road that leads to heaven? The choice is yours. Do you want to pray the sinner's prayer or pray the prayer of sin? Which is bowing your knee to Satan?"

"What is the sinner's prayer? How's that go? Not that I want to pray it right now. It's just so that I know."

"It goes like this." Bruce tells Rubin the prayer anyway, believing that GI will pray that prayer someday.

"Now, GI, don't ever forget that prayer. Just remember that Jesus is knocking at the door of your heart. I pray that you will let him in."

"I gotta go. We talk later."

"Okay, G. Talk to you later."

They both hang up.

GI goes into his room. He sees the small Bible that his probation officer has given him. Then he hears a small voice in head saying, "John 3:16."

He goes to his bed, sits down on it, and picks up the Bible. He takes off his head band and puts it on his nightstand. He opens the Bible to John 3:16. Before he reads it, he remembers himself yelling at Kristal about God hating him. Then he reads out loud to himself, "For God loved the world that He gave His one and only Son, that whoever believes in Him shall not perish but have eternal life."

What's that supposed to mean? he asks himself.

He reads it again. He asks himself the same question. He then begins to read it over and over again until he memorizes it. He starts to think more about the verse. *It can't be true*, he said to himself. He reads the next verse.

"For God did not send His Son into the world to condemn the world, but to save the world through Him."

He thinks about it. He reads it again. *Is this really true?* he asks himself.

"Well, whatever." He puts the Bible down.

GI's mother comes back in the house with Snake's mother and Snake. Snake goes into GI's room. He sees the Bible on the bed and picks it up.

"Man, what you doing with dis?" Snake asks.

"My probation officer wants me to read it."

"What? Man that's bull. What is he? Some kind of pastor evangelist on TV? Preach about the promise land and snatch the money from a nigga's hand. Come over my house, G. I'll hook you up with a good porno mag."

"It didn't hurt to read dat Bible."

"Nigga, what your problem? You been getting too religious on me lately. You know how much I hate them church people."

"Ight. You don't have to dis them."

"What, you become one of 'em?"

"Hell no."

"Well, ight then. Be ready tomorrow. We doing it. I know dat you are going. Ight?"

"Hell yeah! I'm in. We do it for T-Pot and Jackie. What time again?"

"Seven p.m. You know your job. Handel your business."

"Ight. I'll handle my business."

"What you doing now, G?"

"Just chillin'. I'm a little tired right now. Let me get some shut-eye for a while."

"Ight. I see you later," Snake says as he steps out the door and closes it.

GI puts the ceiling fan on in his room. He takes off his gun from his pants and puts it in his nightstand drawer. He takes off his pants and lies down on his bed on his back. He closes his eyes. A few minutes later, he is in a deep sleep.

Monna and Ginalee are in the kitchen. They are just talking away. Snake is out in front of his house with the rest of the gang. An hour goes by.

GI wakes up. He puts his pants on. He reaches into the nightstand drawer and grabs his gun. He tucks the gun under the front inside of his jeans and covers the gun with his shirt. He steps out of his house. He sees the gang. He sees the gang in front of Snake's house and pays no attention to them. He walks to the edge of his property. He turns right and starts walking. He has the Bible in his back pocket. While he is walking, he sees Ice, one of the Majestics, the one who shot T-Pot.

GI gets behind a dumpster. He takes out his .38 and points it at Ice. For some reason, GI can't get a clear shot at Ice. There are a few other guys hanging around Ice, buying drugs from him. One of them keeps getting in front of Ice so that GI can't see.

Ice makes his sales and walks away. GI follows him. GI manages to stay back within fifty feet from Ice and still keep him in view. GI follows Ice all the way to the Majestic hideout. GI ducks behind another dumpster. He thinks for a minute. *All I want is Ice*, GI thinks to himself. *If I call my boyz, they will all kill off the whole gang. I don't want the whole gang. I just want Ice. What do I do?* he thought to himself.

Suddenly, he gets a plan. He comes out from behind the dumpster. He walks right up to the front of the entrance. Two Majestics come out.

"Yo. Waz up?" GI asks.

"Who is you?" one of the Majestics asks.

"Looking fo Ice. Wanna buy some weed."

"You got the dough?"

GI reaches for his wallet. He takes it out. He shows them the money. They let him in. They lead him to where Ice is. Ice is in a room where he is counting his money on a table. GI closes the door behind him as he enters the room. He walks up to the table where Ice is. GI takes out his .38 and points it at Ice's face. GI kicks over the table.

"What the?" Ice asked in fear. "Who the f...f...f..."

"Don't say nothin', nigga! I'm GI, one of the Super Destroyers, cousin of Snake, the leader. Stand up, bi…"

"What you want wit' me?" Ice interrupts.

"Get on the floor, nigga!"

Ice does what he is commanded to do. Ice lies with his stomach on the floor.

"Face up, nigga!"

Ice turns over. Ice is unarmed. His gun is on the other side of the room. His gun flew up in air when GI kicks over the table. GI sits on top of his chest. He puts the barrel of the .38 to Ice's head.

"You killed my homie, nigga! You killed my best friend and girlfriend! Now you gonna die, punk!"

"Who's your friend?" Ice asks, shaking with fear.

"The nigga's name is T-Pot! My girlfriend was Jackie."

"I don't know what you are talking about!"

"Now you gonna die!"

GI shoves the barrel inside Ice's mouth, breaking the front teeth. GI pulls the trigger, and a big *bang* came out of the gun. Somebody kicks the door of the room where they were. GI points the gun at the person who kicked open the door and lets out a shot from the .38 but misses the person. The person who kicked open the door shoots GI right between the eyes with a .45 Magnum. GI falls to the floor dead.

GI wakes up with a cold sweat. He is sitting up and trembling with fear. His bedroom is dark, and he sees the ceiling fan twirling around as he feels the wind from the fan. Then he realizes that it was all a dream. His room is dark and he could hear Ginalee and Mona talking in the kitchen.

He turns the light on. He opens the nightstand drawer and sees that his .38 is still there. He is still shaken up from the dream. He gets out of bed and puts his jeans on. He picks up the phone and sees that Bruce had called him. He dials the phone number and gets the voicemail. He decides not to leave a message and hangs up.

He grabs his .38 and puts it under the front of his pants and covers it with his T-shirt. He walks out of his room. He walks past the kitchen to the front door. He walks out and meets up with the rest of the gang. They all go to a nightclub to hang out.

A few of the Super Destroyers are dancing on the dance floor. Some are picking pockets. Toad and GI meet with some other girls and start to dance on the dance floor. The DJ begins to play some slow rage music. Toad and GI begin to dirty dance with the girls that they have met. This goes on for the rest of the night. At eleven thirty, GI has to leave so that he will not be late with his mother's midnight curfew. Toad gives GI a ride home. It is now quarter to twelve. Toad is in front of GI's house in his car with GI in the front passenger seat.

"GI," Toad says. "Is everything straight with you?"

"Yeah. I'm ight. Everything straight."

"Snake tells me that you been getting religious on us. Having a Bible and all. There's no reason for it to be on you."

"I ain't got no Bible on me. Do you see one on me?"

"I been your homie a long time. You watch yourself tomorrow. I shot four of 'em at that picnic and more cops than I could count. They all deserve to die. Everybody who I kill deserves to die. Only the Destroyers shall live by the gun. Those bastard Christians say that. 'The just shall live by faith.' Man, I say, 'The Destroyers shall live by the almighty gun.' You got to get that killer instinct back in you."

Toad gives GI a bag of crack and a glass pipe.

"Do this tonight. By tomorrow night, you'll be ready for anything. Trust me. It also works for me."

"I can't. I'm on probation. I gotta take a drug test on Saturday."

"Don't worry, man. I'm also on probation. For three years. I still do crack. I get secret piss for the test. I'll take good care of you. Besides that, do it for T-Pot. He would want you to do it anyway."

GI takes the crack and the glass pipe from Toad. "This is for T," GI says. He looks up at the dark sky. "Yo, T. I'm doing this for you. I'll see you tomorrow, Toad. You can jump back into that lily pad by the lake."

GI gets out of the car, and Toad hands him a lighter. GI walks up to his porch and sits on the steps. Toad is in the car lighting up a joint. GI sets up the glass pipe. He lights it up and inhales the pipe. He keeps the smoke inside for a few seconds and breathes it out. He feels himself getting light-headed. Toad is watching from the car.

GI's front door swings open, and his mother comes out. She sees GI sitting on the front step smoking the crack.

"Hey!" she says. "What the hell is going on over here?" she sees the small bag of crack.

"Rubin! Get the hell out of here!"

GI gets up and Toad turns to see what is going on. GI holds the crack pipe in his hands and shows it to her.

"But, Ma, it's only crack. There's nothing wrong with it. I'm not hooked."

"Rubin! You get the hell out of here now! I am throwing you out of here tonight. You go find somewhere else to live. I don't want any crackheads in my house! Go!"

GI runs over to Toad's car.

"Toad, get me outta here!" GI says.

"Get in, G."

GI gets into Toad's car and Toad drives off.

"My mamma kicked me out. Man, I can't believe it," GI says.

"Ight. You can chill out at my crib with Centipede for now. Dat cool with you?"

"Yeah. I'm cool wit' it."

Toad drives home. When they get there, GI lies down on the couch. He takes out the crack pipe again and starts smoking and passes out. The next day, Toad and Centipede wake up GI by throwing a glass of water in his face. GI wakes up and looks at his watch and sees that it is one thirty in the afternoon.

"Yo. Wake up, nigga." Centipede says.

"Yo. What me doing here?" GI asks.

"Off my couch, nigga. I told you, sleep in the bedroom, not my couch," Toad says. "Hardheaded nigga."

"Yo mamma threw you out last night. Dat true?" Centipede asks.

"I on no. Where am I?" GI asks.

"How much crack you smoke last night?"

"I over at Toad's house?"

"You ready for tonight? We gonna kill them Majestics," Toad says. "Snake said to be over at seven. We got time to make some sales. Let's go. GI, we'll meet you at your cousin's house. Ight?"

GI spends the rest of the day at Toad and Centipede's house. He smokes another rock of crack. At six thirty, he starts to walk over to Snake's house. He arrives at Snake's house at seven.

They get into four different cars and drive off with Beast leading the way. The time is now seven thirty in the evening. They all park in a dark alley. Nobody sees or hears them coming. Nobody knows that they were coming.

They all get out of their cars. They hop over a fence that was to the left of them. They go into an empty building that was in front of the Majestics' hide out.

Scorpion and Lizard are sharpshooters. Both go to the top floor. Both have high-powered rifles with night vision scopes and silencers. These guns were given to them by Beast. Scorpion and Lizard set up. They both look through the scopes. They study the building. They notice some lights keeping some of the rooms lit. They can see everybody. Then they see the guards guarding the top of the building.

"Ready?" Lizard whispers.

"I'm ready," Scorpion whispers.

They begin to count together while whispering. "One, two, three."

They both squeeze the triggers at the same time. The bullets go right through each guard's chest. Nobody hears the gunshots at all. Both guards fall to the ground. The rest of the Majestics are inside the building. Scorpion and Lizard go back down to the first floor to meet up with Snake.

"Handle your business, Beast," Snake says.

Beast walks across the street. He walks up to the guards at the main door. Beast knew them and was good friends at one time when Beast was in the Majestics. Beast walks over to them acting friendly.

"Hey yo. What's up, bros?" Beast asks.

"Nigga, I haven't seen you in so long. Where you been at?" one of the guards asks.

"Man. I been all over the United States telling children to stay away from gangs. I came back to see you both."

"That's cool," both guards say together.

"Yeah. What's also cool is that I am now a Super Destroyer."

"WHAT? OH NO!" They cried out as Beast pulls out two .45 Magnums with silencers in each hand. Beast puts both barrels of the guns onto the chests of each guard and pulls the triggers.

The rest of the Super Destroyers see this and come running. They go through the door shooting. Some of the Super Destroyers break windows to get into the building. The Majestics return fire. Lizard sees where Ice went and shows GI. GI goes after him, shooting at some of the Majestics. All the Super Destroyers provide cover for GI, shooting at the Majestics. GI runs around to another floor with Lizard as his backup. Lizard gets shot in the leg twice. GI runs off. He sees Ice running upstairs. He gets free of the gunfire. He runs upstairs after Ice. Ice shoots back. GI returns fire. Ice runs into an empty room and slams the door.

GI sees which room Ice went in. He runs and rams the door with his shoulder. The door breaks open and knocks Ice to the floor, causing Ice's gun to fly out of his hand and over to the other side of the room. GI sees Ice on the floor lying face up. He sits on top of his chest with the barrel of the gun on Ice's head. GI screams and cusses at Ice.

Suddenly, GI hears the words in his head, "'Vengeance is mine,' says the Lord!" Then he heard the words, "Forgive seventy times seven!" When he heard those words in his head, he suddenly backs off and takes the gun off Ice's head.

Then for some unknown reason, GI begins to pray.

"Lord Jesus, I come to you now. I ask for you to forgive me of all my sins. Lord, I believe now and confess that God raised Jesus from the dead. Come into my heart and be my Lord and Savior. Wash me and clean me in your blood. In your name, I pray. Thank you, Lord, for saving me."

After he finishes that prayer, he stands up. He helps Ice to his feet. He looks at Ice and says, "Normally, I would have killed you.

But tonight, I just accepted Jesus into my heart. Now get out of here. I hope to see you in heaven someday."

Just as he said that to Ice, the gang leader of the Majestics walks into the room and shoots GI right in the stomach. GI falls to the floor like a tree. The gang leader gives GI another shot.

Chapter 9

GI lies in an ambulance and is being rushed to a hospital. About two dozen ambulances are being rushed to the hospital. Half of the Super Destroyers and Majestics are shot, wounded, and killed. GI is alive but in critical condition with two bullets in his stomach. When the ambulance gets to the hospital, he is rushed into the emergency room. The rest of the Super Destroyers are at Toad's house.

In the hospital, Beast has a bullet in his head and chest. He is dying. Sticker and Flicker are pronounced DOA on the way to the hospital. Centipede has three bullets in his heart and one in his head, and died instantly in the battle. Lizard has two bullets in his leg and one in his shoulder.

The next day, GI is in an ICU room in coma. His mother is at his bedside in tears. Kristal, Bruce, and Bee Bee walk in. Kristal walks behind GI's mother and puts her hand on her shoulder.

"It's all my fault," Ginalee says. "I never should have kicked him out of the house. I should have seen this coming."

"Don't blame yourself, Mrs. Jackson," Kristal says.

"My son is in ICU. Only if I tried a little harder, he wouldn't be here."

"We all tried, Mrs. Jackson. We all did our best," Kristal says.

Bruce walks over to Ginalee and gets down on one knee beside her. "Mrs. Jackson?" Bruce asks.

Ginalee looks and sees Bruce. "Yes?" she says.

"Do you remember me?" Bruce asks.

"Not so sure."

"I went by the name Junkblood," he says softly.

Ginalee sobs and nods her head. "Yes. I remember you. I heard that you were dead. Where have you been?"

"I quit the gangsta lifestyle. Well, God delivered me from it. I gave Rubin my testimony. I am a changed man. Changed by the power of the Holy Ghost."

"How?"

Bruce gives his testimony. An hour goes by. Ginalee is very touched by Bruce's testimony.

"Do you want us to pray for you and Rubin?" Bruce asks.

"Yes. I congratulate you for getting out of the gang. Please pray for my son. I have to get to work now. Please call me if he gets out of this coma. Here is my cell number."

Ginalee writes it down on a hospital notepad and leaves it on the table next to GI's bed.

"We will call you."

Ginalee gets up and gives them all hugs, then walks out the door.

"God bless you, Mrs. Jackson," Bruce says as Ginalee walks out the door.

"I knew this would happen," Kristal says. "Let's pray for GI right now."

They all get up and get around GI's bed and hold hands. Bruce begins to speak in an unknown language. They follow after Bruce. Then Bruce begins to pray, "Lord Jesus, we come to you now. We ask that you reach down and save Rubin. We ask that you would deliver him out of the bondage of this gang lifestyle. Touch him right now, Lord. Lay your healing hands on Rubin right now and take him out of this coma. Holy Spirit, we ask that you would move right now. We ask that you would fill up this room right now. We ask that you would let Jesus be glorified in this place. Touch us all. If it is God's will for Rubin to die, we ask that you would start a revival through this. In the name of Jesus, we all touch and agree that God's will be done. In the name of Jesus Christ, we pray. Amen."

"*Ba.*" They all hear a sound out of GI's mouth. "*Ba, ba, ba.*"

"GI," Kristal says. "We are all here for you."

GI starts to wake up. He opens his eyes slowly. He sees Kristal, Bee Bee, and Bruce standing around his bed. "Where am I?" he barely asks in a painful voice.

"GI," Bruce says softly. "You are in a hospital. Can you hear us?"

"Junk?" GI asks painfully as he looked at Bruce.

"Yeah. It's me. Old Junkblood."

"What am I doing here?"

"You were shot in the stomach."

GI is feeling some very intense pain from his stomach going down below his waist. He is able to move his head, arms, and legs.

Suddenly, Sergeant Richard Butler walks into the hospital room with Probation Officer Sean Walker. They see GI in the bed.

"Well, what do we have here?" Sean asks.

"Do you know him?" Kristal asks.

"You Pastor Butler, right?" Bruce asks as he looks at Sergeant Butler.

"Yes, I am," Sergeant answers. "This is Sean Walker. He is Rubin's probation officer. How do you know me? I'm actually one of the pastors of my church."

"You've come to my church many times to preach," Bruce answers. "You go to Grace Tab, right?"

"Yes, I do. What church do you go to?"

"Holy Revival. What brings you two here?"

"Police work. How is Pastor Blanchard?"

"He's doing great. Praising the Lord, preaching the Word, and living for the Lord."

"We had a great service on Sunday," Kristal says. "Rubin came too. I picked him up"

"Really?" Richard says. "Hey, Rubin. You got to go to church?"

"Yeah," GI says softly. "I really enjoyed it."

"You did?" Richard asks.

"But you didn't get saved. That's why we are here. What were you doing last night?" Sean asks.

"I got shot," GI answers painfully.

"We know you got shot," Richard says. "Why did you get shot?"

"Someone opened the door. Then he shot me."

"Who shot you?"

"Don't know his name."

"Tell us where you were and why you were there."

GI is in too much pain to say much. "But I didn't kill Ice. I began to pray."

"You?" Sean asks. That last statement by GI catches him off guard. "What did you pray?"

"I asked Jesus to come into my heart."

"*What?*" everyone asks at the same time.

"For…real," GI says painfully. "I helped Ice to his feet. Then I said to him, 'I forgive you.' Then I got shot. For the last half hour, I kept hearing the words, 'You will be with me in Paradise forever' in my head."

Bruce has his Bible with him. He opens it to Luke 23:43. Suddenly, a chill fell on Bruce and his body shook after he read that verse. "Oh my God," Bruce says. "Those are the words of Jesus to the thief who hung next to him when he was being crucified. Glory to God! Rubin is saved!"

"Praise the Lord!" Kristal shouts with tears going down her face.

Suddenly, the doctor walks in. Doctor Stevens is a tall white man with short black hair. He has been a doctor for twenty years at the hospital and is a UCLA graduate. He looks at the medical report on the bed. Doctor Stevens checks GI's pulse, heartbeat, and temperature.

"Hello. I am Doctor Stevens."

"What's his condition, doc?" Sean asks.

"Are you his probation officer?" Doctor Stevens asks.

"Yes, I am. Sean Walker." Sean extends his hand and they both shake hands.

"Well," Doctor Stevens says. "He got shot with an exploding bullet. We can't do anything to take the bullet out unless the swelling in his liver goes down which might cause his liver to deteriorate. In other words, if the swelling goes down in his liver, he might end up having that thing with the NFL running back had with his hip. You know, the running back who played for Los Angeles? What's his name? That could be fatal."

"What could happen if you don't remove the bullet in time?" Bruce asks.

"If we don't remove the bullet in time, it could lead into internal bleeding, which will be even more fatal. The explosion from the bullet did some serious damage to his abdominal area. We are still running some more tests. He was shot twice. The first bullet hit his liver. The second hit his stomach. Both can cause internal bleeding. We are doing everything to save him. This is the ICU. Many people die here."

"Well, if he does die," Richard said, "at least he dies with Jesus Christ."

Bee Bee comes back into the room. "Rubin's mother is on her way. So is Pastor Blanchard."

A half hour later, while everyone is fellowshipping in GI's room, Ginalee walks in.

"Rubin?" she asks. "Are you all right?"

"Mom," GI says. "I am so sorry," he says in pain. "Got saved. I accepted Jesus Christ last night."

"That's great, baby. I'm glad that you did something right," Ginalee says.

Ten minutes later, Pastor Blanchard walks in. Everybody greets him with a hug. Pastor David looks at GI. "My son, I don't know what you got yourself into. But Jesus Christ is the only way out."

"He got saved last night," Bruce says.

"Praise God. You must be the boy's mother," Pastor David says to Ginalee.

"Yes, I am," she said. "I am his mother."

They stay for the rest of the day and evening with GI and his mother. Pastor David and Bruce minister to them and pray for them. Through this, Ginalee gets saved. Visiting hours come to an end. Before everyone leaves, they pray one last time. Then GI quotes John 3:16 to Sean Walker. Pastor David goes down to the gift shop and buys GI and Ginalee new NIV study Bibles. Bruce gives Ginalee a ride home.

The next day, Toad and Snake come to visit GI. When they come to visit, they see him reading the new Bible that Pastor David bought for him. They get angry.

"Yo," Snake said. "What the hell are you reading this for?" he snatches it from GI and gives it to Toad.

"I'll get rid of this thing," Toad says. He drops it in the trash can.

"Yo," GI says painfully. "Why you do that?"

"What? You want that shi—"

Toad is about to say when Bruce walks into the room. Bruce is just getting off work. He is dressed in a black dress shirt and pants while wearing a white tie. Bruce walks over to the trash can. He takes the Bible out of the trash can and gives it back to GI.

"That was unnecessary, Toad," Bruce says. "Freedom of religion. He is allowed to read it."

"Junkblood?" Toad asks. "Is dat you?"

"It's me, man," Bruce says. "Alive well. Delivered and set free. Changed by the power of the Holy Ghost."

"What?" Snake asks. "Man, you did change. I thought you were dead."

Bruce starts to give his testimony to Snake and Toad. An hour goes by, Bruce shows them the scars on his arms from the needles. He tells how God is using the needle marks as a testimony to other kids to stay away from gangs and drugs.

"So, you be dis sellout that my cousin told me about. You sold us out," Snake says.

"Look, Snake," Bruce says. "It's either God's way out or in a body bag. Which way do you prefer?"

"You know what?" Toad asks. "I see what you mean. Now I understand. You needed to find some way to get off that needle. I understand why you left. I respect that."

"Well, Toad," Bruce says. "It's not about me. It's all about Jesus. It's not by might. Nor by power. But my spirit, says the Lord. It's only in Jesus where you will find freedom. Being in the gang was like being in hell. I was always looking over my shoulder to see if someone was going to kill me."

"Snake," Rubin says. "He's right. I was a lot like that. That's why I got saved."

"*What?* Snake asks in disbelief.

78

Toad stands there speechless.

"I can't take any more."

"I don't know what you have towards Jesus. But there's nothing wrong," GI says.

"I'm outta here," Snake says, then he walks out the room.

Toad stands there with his back against the wall and can't speak. Finally, he manages to speak. "Yo, what the hell did you do to my homie?"

"I didn't do anything," Bruce says.

"You lie mother fu—"

"It's true, Toad," GI interrupted. "He didn't do anything to me. It's all about Jesus."

"Jesus?" Toad asks. "Jesus was some nigga who wants to condemn all the niggas of the world."

"That's not true, Toad," Rubin says. "Jesus loves you. Jesus did not come to this world to condemn you. He came to save you."

"Jesus did not come to call the righteous but only the sinner," Bruce says. "The Bible says that, 'The wages of sin is death.' But the gift of God is eternal life through Jesus Christ. our Lord."

Toad thinks about it for a while. Snake has gone home. He doesn't want to hear anymore about Jesus. He has seen a lot of religious hypocrisy while growing up. Toad is now by himself in the ICU room with Bruce and GI.

"Toad," Bruce says. "If you walk out that door this very second, I can't guarantee that you will come back alive tomorrow. But I can promise that if you stay in this room for a while, you will receive the gift of eternal life through Jesus Christ."

"I know what you have been through. I know it was hard growing up. It was hard for me too. But one thing I know is that Jesus can heal you of all that you have been through. There is healing in his hands. I can't heal you. GI can't heal you. There's no pastor, bishop, or evangelist that can heal you or save you. It's only through Jesus Christ. Jesus took the weight of the whole world on his shoulders. He also took the sins of the whole world upon himself. God the Father even turned his back on Jesus when he hung on that cross. He was the final sacrifice for sin. Jesus is able to forgive us of all of our sins. Do you want to know this Jesus?"

Toad thinks for a minute.

I don't think Jesus could ever forgive me for what I have done in life, Toad thinks. *Could this Jesus be so loving and forgiving? My life is so messed up. Who can set my life straight?*

"Whoever this Jesus is," Toad says to Bruce, "can he really put my life straight? Can he really heal my past?"

"Absolutely, bro. If he can do it for me, then he sure can do it for you."

"Then how do I get to know this Jesus?"

"Toad, my friend, do you want to accept Jesus into your heart and become born-again? I'm talking about a new creation in Christ."

"Yes," Toad says with his eyes filling up with moisture.

Bruce gives Toad a hug. Toad returns the hug. Toad starts to have tears go down his face. "I want to know this Jesus," Toad says.

Bruce puts his hand on Toad's shoulder and leads him into the sinner's prayer. With every sentence that Toad says, he has tears going down his face. Thirty seconds later, Toad becomes a brand-new creation in Christ. Then GI's mother walks into the room. She sees Toad and sees the tears going down his cheeks. She pauses and looks in disbelief with joy.

"It's okay, Mrs. Jackson," Bruce says. "Toad just got saved."

"Hi, Mom," GI says.

"Hi, baby," Ginalee says. "How you feeling?"

"I'm starting to feel pain all over. Now I am starting to feel something right here." GI puts his hand on his stomach. "It is starting to hurt even more right now. Get the doctor!"

Bruce goes out the room. He runs to the nurse's station and gets a nurse. The nurse comes running back. GI starts feeling more pain. Suddenly, he starts coughing and spitting up blood. More nurses and Doctor Stevens come running into the room. Toad, Bruce, and Ginalee are ordered to wait outside. Ten minutes later, Doctor Stevens walks out GI's room. He walks up to Ginalee.

"Mrs. Jackson," Dr. Stevens says. "I'm so sorry. We did everything we could to save him. He died." He walks away sadly.

"No! Nooo!" Ginalee cries out.

Ginalee stands in the hallway with her arms around Bruce and Toad. She is crying hysterically in their arms. Bruce begins to pray for her. Bruce does what he can to minister to her.

"He's with Jesus now. He will be with Jesus forever," Bruce says.

Bruce takes Ginalee home after she takes one last look at her son. Rubin Jackson, a.k.a. GI, dies in his hospital bed due to internal bleeding from two bullets to his abdomen.

The next week is Rubin's funeral at Holy Revival Ministries. Pastor David hosts the service. Ginalee has asked him to host the service. The rest of the gang who are still alive are at the funeral. Pastor David preaches a great inspiring message. Ginalee and Monna sits in the front row. Kristal sings the hymn "Because He Lives."

Chapter 10

The next week, Toad comes over to Snake's house. Snake comes outside. He greets Toad with a hug.

"Snake, my brother," Toad said, "we need to talk."

"What's up?" Snake asks. "Have not seen you in a while. I been by your house and you not home anymore."

"I wanted to wait after GI's funeral to talk with you. By the way, I prefer you call me Charley. My name is Charley Smith."

"Yeah. I know dat. Why the sudden change?"

"Because I'm a changed man. I know that I been avoiding your calls and text messages. But I needed some space between us and the gang. You know how loyal I been. I am always there when you need me. You see, I've been staying with Bruce. You know Junkblood?

"He's been ministering to me, and I have been going through biblical counseling. I became a born-again Christian the day that GI died. It happened right before he died. So he got to see me get saved. Bruce led me in a prayer that gave me a personal relationship with Jesus Christ. That's why I am here, Snake. I want out of the gang."

"What the fu... ?"

"Snake, I'm serious," Charley cuts him off.

Snake gets very angry.

"You born-again bastard! What's gotten into you?"

"It's Jesus that is in me now. I got rid of all my weapons and ammo. I threw them into the ocean when I went fishing on Bruce's uncle's fishing boat with Bruce."

"I don't believe what I am hearing. Nigga, you are a stupid mother fu..."

"Snake, I am leaving. Goodbye. Jesus loves you, and I will be praying for you." Toad turns around to walk away.

"You won't be praying for me, nigga." Snake takes out his .357 and points it at Toad's back. "Your prayers end right now bit."

A loud *bang* sound comes out of Snake's .357, and a flash goes out of the barrel. Toad falls to the ground. He is shot in the back from five feet away.

*****

Hours later, Charley is in the hospital. He gets through the surgery and is in the recovery room. Bruce and Pastor David are with him. Charley wakes up. Snake is in jail. When Charley wakes up, he is very groggy.

"Charley?" Bruce asks. "You okay?"

"Yeah," Charley answers. "What happened?"

"Snake is in jail. He shot you," Bruce answers.

Charley goes back to sleep. He wakes up the next day around noon. He sees Bruce standing by his bedside with Bee Bee. On the other side of the bed, he sees Kristal. In front of his bed, he sees Richard Butler in LAPD uniform.

"Charley Smith?" Richard asks. "Is your name Charley Smith?"

"Yes it is," Charley answers, waking up.

"Do you know that a Jamal Jackson, who goes by the street name Snake, is the one who shot you?"

"Yes," Charley answers. "Is he in jail?"

"Yes he is. If you wish to press charges by testifying against him, he could be facing thirty to fifty years in prison for attempted murder. Do you wish to testify?"

"No. I forgive him. I want those charges to drop."

"Are you out of your mind, bro?" Bruce asks.

"Are you sure?" Richard asks.

"God told me in a dream last night. I saw him and me preaching and ministering to the rest of the gangs in LA. I woke up with God telling me to forgive Snake. It was like the weirdest thing. It's like, I know this is God. I just kept hearing him telling me to drop these charges and to forgive Snake for shooting me."

Later that day, Snake is released from jail. He hears about Charley forgiving him and dropping the charges against him. The police report is changed from attempted murder to accidental usage of firearm. Charley stays in the hospital for another six weeks going through rehab and therapy to learn how to walk again. Each day, Snake and Bruce would visit him in the hospital, and Charley would minister the love of Jesus to Snake. Snake is very hard-hearted at first. But as time goes on, Snake would listen and be more open to hear what Charley is saying.

In the sixth week, Charley is in his hospital room having lunch with Pastor David. Snake walks into the room. He sits on the other chair next to the bed.

"You know, Toad—excuse me, Charley," Snake says. "I now see how much Jesus loves me. I saw too much religious hypocrisy growing up. If this Jesus is as loving and caring as you say that he is, then I want to know him for myself."

"Well, praise the Lord!" Pastor David says. "Can I lead you into a prayer or would you like Charley to do it?"

Charley leads Snake into a prayer. Thirty seconds later, Snake becomes a new creation in Christ. Charley and Pastor David both pray for Snake. After they pray for Snake, Pastor David goes to the hospital gift shop and buys Snake a brand-new NIV study Bible.

The next day, Charley is released from the hospital. He is given some assignments to help his therapy to strengthen his legs and back. They get into Pastor Blanchard's car with Charley in the back seat. They drive over to Ginalee's house. She is sitting on a patio chair on the front porch, reading her Bible and listening to some gospel music.

When the car stops in front of Ginalee's house, Snake and Pastor David step out of the car. Snake opens the back seat door for Charley and helps him out of the car. They go over to Ginalee, and they all great her with a hug. Ginalee puts her hands on Snake's head and prays for him. Pastor David gets behind him. Snake falls back, and Pastor David catches him and gently puts Snake on the floor.

Ten minutes later, Snake gets back up. They fellowship for about an hour. Monna, who is now saved, comes outside the house.

She sees them at Ginalee's house. She walks over to her house to join them. They had a time of worship to welcome Charley home.

Later on in the week, while Charley, Bruce, and Snake are at Snake's house, Rod and Cruz comes over. They are so surprised to see Bruce alive. Bruce and Charley gives them his testimony. Charley starts to tell them about how he is able to forgive Snake for shooting him. Snake testifies about the love of Jesus Christ and what Jesus has done on the cross. On that day, Cruz and Rod accept Christ.

Revival begins to spread throughout the rest of the gang. Two weeks later, what is left of the Super Destroyers is saved through the power of the Holy Spirit. Three weeks later, the gang is on stage at holy revival, giving their testimonies of what Jesus has done for them. They change their name from Super Destroyers to Demon Destroyers. They are very much supported by holy revival. They are now used by God to minister to other gangs in the Los Angeles area.

Epilogue

If you are ever passing through this area and looking for a place to spend the night, be sure to stay at Snake and his new gang. Then you will really receive a blessing from the hood.

The events and characters in this story are all fictitious. However, this book is based on the real lives of street gangs.

To all the gangs, my heart goes out to you all.

If you are looking for a way out of all your troubles, always remember that Jesus is right there for you. He loves you and wants to set you free. If you want to be set free from your sins and have Jesus save you, then pray this following prayer.

Lord Jesus, I come to you now. Lord Jesus, I am a sinner. Forgive me of all of my sins. Wash me and cleanse me with your blood. Come into my heart and be my Lord and Savior. I believe in my heart and confess with my mouth that God raised Jesus from the dead so that I can be saved. I thank you, Jesus, for saving me. I declare that from this day forward, I am saved. I am a new creation in you. In the name of Jesus, I pray. Amen.

About the Author

Born and raised in New York and living in South Florida since 1995, Philip Allisson is now writing his first novel, *Blessings from da Hood*. After watching movies like *Colors*, *Boyz in the Hood*, and *Menace II Society*, Philip Allisson felt a calling to write a novel about gangs. He wanted to reach out to gangs all around the world. In this book, he dedicates this novel to those who live the thug life and to those who have been redeemed from the gangsta lifestyle.